WAITING TO BE FED

Authored by

D. R. B. TARR & VOU PAM

Waiting To Be Fed

For information, please address any requests to:

SoniaVou Books Subsidiary Rights

Published by SoniaVou Books LLC

Houston, Texas

info@soniavoubooks.com

For online orders and information, please visit:

www.waitingtobefed.com

Your comments are welcome.

ISBN: 978-0-9824497-6-9 Perfectbound

ISBN: 978-0-9824497-5-2 eBook

ISBN: 978-0-9824497-7-6 Hardcover with Jacket

Cover concept by Oludotun Olukoya

Cover and Interior design by CreateSpace

DEDICATION

To every man and woman who stands,
or ever stood, for justice and the cause of humanity.

CONTENTS

THE ASSIGNMENT

My name is Carl Fergusson Jr.; an American of Jamaican descent, I was born in New York in the early seventies. Even though I was not old enough to experience the horrors and struggles that defined the era of the Civil Rights Movement, I heard so many gory stories about the era from some of those who did.

Fear no man or woman, my dad used to say, but you must fear God. The fear of God, he explained, was not about being frightened of God, but about being careful not to incur the displeasure of a loving and benevolent Father. He urged me never to allow fear to rule my life because fear is the food of the devil. This was one of three things he wanted me to develop as principles behind any decisions that I make in life, or any course of actions on which I choose to embark. The other two were that I must endeavor to speak the truth at all times, and also to defend the truth always, even at the cost of my life. At the time, I did not know just how tall an order all that would be. I was just a little over eleven years old when we first had that conversation. Over the years, he reinforced it at every opportunity. The sad thing was that I never got a chance to enjoy his pep talks for several years before he died.

If I had the opportunity, I would have suggested to him that I came to the conclusion that ignorance is the food and tool of the devil, not fear. Ignorance, actually, is what breeds fear, along with the prejudices that prevent greater unity and progress within the global human community. It is like a cancer – ignorance, that is – that grows and spreads across generations of the human race except when and where it is aggressively checked by the attainment of knowledge. Most times, rather unfortunately, many of us learn the most important lessons of life too late, and often in extremely harsh ways.

My dad had recently died, and I am just coming to terms with his passing. It was hurting a lot more than I thought it would. We all saw it coming, of course. He had been battling heart disease for quite a while, but I guess there is no amount of preparation that really gets one ready for that final moment.

He had asked if he could come over to my place for the weekend to relax a little bit and watch the football playoffs with me. He was an avid supporter of the Pittsburgh Steeler's. We had a good lunch, settled down comfortably on the sofa and enjoyed the game. Dad picked up the cable remote control to flip through the news channels. He always loved to remain current with global news and events.

All of a sudden, he complained of an itchy sensation along his arms and wondered aloud what could possibly have been the cause of his unfolding discomfort. My wife expressed the probability of an allergic reaction, thereby suggesting the use of some antihistamine while we figured out the cause of the reaction. No sooner had I gotten up to get the antihistamine, I noticed his speech had become slurred, while the TV remote control slipped from a right hand suddenly gone limp. In the twinkling of an eye, his mouth was drooping on one side of his face.

From the little information shared by friends in the medical field, I figured immediately that he had just suffered a stroke. We called 911 and it seemed like an eternity before the ambulance arrived. I rode in the ambulance in which dad was rushed to the Emergency Room, while my wife followed later in her car after making arrangements for a neighbor to take care of the kids.

There he was – unconscious – totally oblivious of what was going on around him. It was hard to believe that just a moment ago, he had been cheering the Steelers and sipping his favorite drink of freshly squeezed organic lemons in ice-cold water. The ER doctor said the scans revealed a massive hemorrhage and he would require surgery.

The surgery was successful. Dad regained consciousness, even though he lost motor functions on the right side of his body and still slurred his speech. He recovered slowly and was able to crack visitors up with a few jokes when they eventually figured out what he was saying. His memory was affected to some extent, but he could still remember some people and recall some past events.

Memories are like a well or bank which hold or save our entire life experiences. It is from there that we draw valuable information that helps us to cope, in one form or another, with all that life continues to throw at us. It gives me the shudders to imagine that something, or anything, can just wipe away a person's lifetime of memories. Like Alzheimer's, for instance, sufferers cannot recognize old friends, close members of their own family – not even their spouses or children, and certainly not themselves. Worse still, Alzheimer sufferers cannot even remember how to do the most basic things they used to do quite routinely. Health is wealth, they say, but most of us never fully appreciate the depth of its meaning.

Sadly, dad had another major stroke while he was still in the hospital. The doctors had forewarned us about the high probability of this occurring. Well, it did, and so quickly too. This time, unfortunately, he did not survive it. Thank goodness, however, that there were some lucid moments before everything went blank for him. Those moments, short as they were, were just so special and so precious. During those 'oh-so-terribly-short' moments, we got closer than we ever did.

Now, officially, I am an orphan. My mother died many years back when I was still a little kid. The story was that she had been in an accident and had suffered terrible injuries from which she later died. Over the years, I picked up a few tidbits from close family members that suggested the story was not true. At some point, I heard that she had committed suicide. Dad angrily denounced the story as rubbish even before I had finished asking him about it. He never told me the entire story surrounding her death until he got very sick. That was one of the few times I had seen that tough old man in tears.

Mother, he said, had committed suicide after being brutally raped and badly beaten by a group of young men. I asked if the young men were ever apprehended and brought to justice, but he only smiled and said, " One way or another, justice will be served by God regardless of how our earthly laws deal with our actions in this world. I've forgiven them all, son. It was very hard, but I forgave them all. Whether or not God judged me guilty for not being unable to protect my wife from the evil that crushed her spirit and desire to go on living, I wish I could forgive myself. It is my prayer that I shall see her sometime soon in the afterlife to apologize in person." Dad did not disclose any information about the perpetrators, or if he even knew who they were. With the kind of wry grin on his face, I believe he knew a whole lot more than he cared to share with me.

On this particular day, I had just gotten back home from dropping off our son at school to settle down for a quick breakfast with my wife. Unlike before, however, the past few mornings had been different, and my wife had noticed that I was unusually distracted. For someone who she always accused of being stuck on CNN day and night, she observed that I was flipping through the local and national news

stations just like my dad used to. On a couple of occasions she asked if I was searching for anything in particular.
Nothing really, was my answer. The truth was that there was
so much going through my mind, and I was simply trying to
figure how to order my next steps.

I am sure my wife, Tueremi, felt confident she knew what
had been giving me sleepless nights for about a week. As
far as she was concerned, my father's passing was having a
much greater effect on me than she had imagined it would.
In a way, Tueremi was right, but she was far from putting
her finger on what the real issue was. It was not my dad's
death that threw me into those pensive moods as much as
what I discovered going through his personal documents
and belongings.

Emerging right before my eyes, through mounds of paper
and other personal effects, was a totally different side of my
dad that I knew absolutely nothing about. I read letters and
documents, saw little keepsakes, and heard the playback of
old and new cassette tapes that gave a totally different perspective of the man I grew up to know as my father. He had
kept a detailed memoir of events in his life, including com-
mentaries about local and international politics. The only
part of his records that was left purposely vague was the
circumstances leading up to my mother's death. He actually
said a lot without saying enough to satisfy my curiosity.

During one of his lucid moments, dad told me where to
find the key to his safety deposit box in the bank, and also
gave me the combination to the little fire-proof safe he kept

at home. With a huge smile, he said to me, "It's about time I gave you a proper introduction to an old buddy of mine known as the Black White Man. It will give me the greatest peace and joy if you would help me keep a promise I made to him many years ago."

That was how dad made me commit to finishing up and publishing a book he had been trying to write for as long as I could remember. Of course, I did not hesitate to make him that promise, and with all sincerity too.

Yes, many times I heard him mention the Black White Man with fondness during the many discussions on race and politics that came up whenever his old buddies and family members came around for a game of dominoes and Gin Rummy.

Among many curios in his safety deposit box, there was an exquisitely decorated hand-made A4-sized leather folder, with a mixture of hand-written and typed but unbound papers, all held together by a leather strap. I recognized the hand-written material to belong to dad, and the volume of material represented a significant effort towards putting a book together. On a number of pages and on a few loose sheets also, were notes written in beautiful cursive. The typed papers, obviously created from those fancy old IBM type-writers, turned out to be a manuscript authored by someone called Thomas Parsons.

In his safe at home, kept in an old leather diary, was a bunch of letters tied in yellow ribbon and a few dried-out roses. The content of the letters spoke of a time, and of a couple who were deeply in love with each other. There was a cardboard box containing a number of well-labeled cassette tapes, two cassette player/recorders, and a digital recorder I had given him for his last birthday, among other interesting items.

When dad entrusted me with this project not too long ago, I must admit that I did not get to it for some time. Now, considering the subject of the tapes and manuscripts, I wish I had taken a keener interest earlier on when dad had talked about working on a book he was trying to get published. The more I listened to the material recorded on those tapes and learned from his notes, the more curious I became to find out more about my dad's earlier life.

There was also this eerie feeling that came over me whenever I listened to the voices in the recordings. I knew, from dad's meticulous notes, that every single one of the people whose voices were on the tapes had died. So, maybe it was my imagination, but I could not help feeling that I felt some kind of presence each time I played back those tapes. Regardless, there was no doubt in my mind that the events described in the manuscripts and audio recordings merited being published into a book.

I was engrossed in the tapes and manuscripts for over six months, trying to research or confirm information contained therein. At the same time, I was giving our local and international communities a closer look from perspectives which I had never stopped long enough to consider. Clearly, I never had a clue just how much of an activist dad was, until I became familiar with the material he had left behind. It would have been great if he was still alive to answer a few of my questions, though.

However, Dad's manuscript was quite detailed. Thomas Parsons' amazingly detailed accounts filled in any gaps that might have been contained in dad's memoirs. Altogether, you could say that the memoirs of these old activists gave a pretty clear picture of the event that had a great impact on their lives.

The closer I got to getting these accounts published into a book, and the more I looked at events unfolding across our country these days, the clearer it became that I was getting dangerously close to taking a dive into the deep end of a massive pool of controversy that could change the course of my hitherto quiet life quite dramatically.

As dad used to say, there is probably no better medium to observe both the follies and incredible potentials of the human race other than on television, courtesy of the mind-numbing number of channels. Without a purpose-driven life and will-power, people could easily spend a quarter of their entire lives (an average of six hours per day) just surfing through television channels these days, watching one program after another.

Trending on different media formats – television, radio, internet, and newspapers – around the world was the tragic shooting death of a seventeen year old unarmed African American boy in Sanford, Florida. While this is being described by many as a racially-motivated crime, his killer claims that he acted in self-defense. The way the African

American community and many sympathizers see it, another young life has been lost. Probably because of the shooter's last name, the conclusion was initially drawn that a young Black man's dreams had been terminated by a "White man" because of the combination of his skin color and stereotyped manner of clothing. The manner of clothing, a hoodie, apparently made the teenager look suspicious to the man who killed him.

The incident sparked off a tinderbox of suppressed emotions and memories of a nightmarish past in African American history, and the perception of a continued targeting of blacks by a White-dominated society. The bottled-up rage about racial prejudice had erupted before it became evident that the shooter was not "a White man" after all, but bi-racial. As if that was not enough, it was further revealed that the shooter's grandfather was a Black man.

While the nation waited to see what further investigation reveals, the incident brought to light the fact that old wounds had not healed, and that there was still a lot of bitterness and distrust among the stakeholders of the American community. Under normal circumstances, our organization would have gone headlong into this. Unfortunately, we have much more trouble on our hands than we can handle right now. Regardless, many of us have resolved to help any way we can.

Rush Limbaugh must have breathed a sigh of relief as the national spotlight was shifted from him to follow the events unfolding in Sanford, Florida. With characteristically unsavory comments, this time around he further fuelled what has been described as a 'war on women' by the Republican Party. For those who hate his guts, it seemed that an opportunity had presented itself for another 'Don Imus event'. There was a huge clamor, justifiably or not, to silence the prolific Radio Talk Show host who also happens to be the loudest voice of the Party.

It never ceases to amaze me, in this day and age, how men continue to imagine that women would not be capable enough to determine what is best for them. From films to shows made to empower women on television and radio networks, none of them is likely to have the desired impact on how women are perceived by men until society reviews and redefines the perspective of most religions regarding the female gender.

Imagine how long it took for men to consider women qualified or capable to vote and participate in the political affairs of the same communities of which they form the cornerstones and bedrock. Now, our male lawmakers have taken it upon themselves to determine and prioritize what matters the most to women regarding female personal health issues and psychological well-being.

Going back to the power of television, even though I had an early morning appointment, I remember being glued to the History2 channel till about two in the morning. I was watching a documentary on President Barack Obama and the events leading up to the successful mission in Pakistan that eliminated the threat posed to the world by its most wanted terrorist, Osama bin Laden.

Then there were the Republican Presidential debates and the race to find a candidate that would be strong enough to defeat President Barack Obama in the fall 2012 Presidential elections. Over the years, it has always been interesting to see how religion is brought into play when it comes to electing the President of the United States. On one hand this time around, some Christian leaders have suggested that President Obama is actually a Muslim at heart, and not the Christian he claims to be. On the other hand, Mitt Romney, a member of the Jesus Christ of Latter Day Saints Church, is not Christian enough because this particular denomination of Christianity to which he belongs (Mormon) is not accepted by mainline Christianity. This interpretation, of course, is that of the leadership of the Christian religion who ultimately determine the criteria that qualify a person or group as Christian or otherwise. It seems to matter very little to most members of the country's mostly Christian leadership and community whether or not an individual has built a record of stewardship to his or her fellow men, women and community – just as Jesus Christ demanded of His followers.

Now that Mitt Romney is on course to be the Republican Party nominee for the Presidential elections in the fall, it appears self-dubbed mainstream Christians may have to 'pinch their noses' (as suggested by a member of the Christian leadership) if he is the one for whom they ultimately decide to cast their votes. Their other choice, however, is to vote for Barack Obama – the man whose faith or religious leaning some still question.

It does make one wonder, at the end of the day, if making the choice for leadership (at all levels) of this great country is really still based on whosoever will deliver the best service, leadership and protection of values which will sustain the greatness of this country.

While on the subject of not being 'enough' of something or the other, President Obama is not considered Black enough for African-Americans and not White enough for Caucasians. And, in a nation where Jim Crow laws are supposed to be long dead and buried (illegal to be applied in any shape or form, that is), it is more than curious that an individual who is half-white and half-black, like President Obama is, should be conveniently referred to as a Black man, and not as a White man. After all, he is fifty percent as White as he is Black.

Each time I brought home a form from school to be filled by my parents, I remember how dad would draw my attention to the boxes that had to be checked. According to him, "one has to be careful not to be psychologically railroaded into being put in a 'box' where they don't belong." Even if you do not have much of a choice on regular forms, he always said, "you must always know who and what you are in this life, and must never allow anyone to determine in which of their predetermined 'boxes' your life must be lived or judged."

As dad said in one of our conversations not long before he passed, it appears the 'one-drop rule' still lives and applies in the minds of many; particularly in the minds of most of the country's lawmakers who one would imagine ought to know much better. According to him, the situation is not helped when one as intellectually sound as President Obama sees and refers to himself as a Black man, even though he clearly belongs to a growing unique set of humans who bear no "traditional" colors. Maybe for him, dad said, it was just a matter of expediency to get the support and votes required to secure the most coveted job in the world. He suggested that President Obama probably just heeded Jesus Christ's advice to be gentle as a dove and wise as a serpent.

With a mischievous smile on my face, I asked him two questions that always got him scratching his balding head, staring briefly into the distance at nothing in particular, and chuckling as he tried to respond. The first question: What are the chances that Dr. Martin Luther King Jr., who lived and died as an active member of the Republican Party, would have become a Democrat had he not been assassinated? After all, almost all those with whom he stood on the Republican Party platform are now avowed members of the same Democratic Party against which they fought a long and painful battle. The second question: Which of the Parties in the American political arena supports the message of Jesus Christ?

Dad admitted that those questions were definitely a whole lot easier to answer many years ago than in current times. Why? The Republican Party historically favored and fought for the freedom of Black people in this country, and stood more for Christian values than the Democratic Party did. Jesus called on humankind to love one another, and not to do unto others what they would not like to be done unto them. He also preached that society should make men independent so that they could fend for themselves and their families, and not made to be solely dependent on others. Along the road to freedom, dad said, the Republican Party represented those values that were deemed necessary for the success of the Black struggle. But, how do yesterday's views and goals stand against the reality of current times and our attempt at a projection for an indeterminable future?

Jesus, dad continued, was favorably disposed to sharing, but vehemently opposed to any type of exploitation. And, although He also supported the distribution of the common wealth of our communities to care for and support the weak and under-privileged, He made it clear that there is a lot of integrity in striving to make a contribution, however little, to the common wealth of one's community. Dad never really drew or arrived at any conclusions.

"That's the thing about time and life, son. When combined, time and life form a huge and seemingly unpredictable force that never stops moving – evolving, so to speak – and always compelling humanity to make urgent and pertinent decisions that call for a redefinition of our perspectives, values and priorities. The changes that I have witnessed in the span of just about fifty years, across all sections of our society, have often left me both speechless and in complete amazement. These kinds of adverse changes are enough to make any man or woman swing positions probably more than once in a lifetime."

It has been said by many that the use of race for political advantage has been more a matter of expediency for Blacks. This school of thought suggests that Black leaders have access to enough historical facts to teach young Black men and women the bare-knuckle truth about the journey from slavery to freedom. Slavery and slave trading were deeply entrenched in the African mindset and way of life long before, and long after, the West came to feature on the scene. The participation of Western nations, for whatever reasons, does not make White people any guiltier than those chieftains of the various communities in Africa, who were more than willing partners in the capturing and selling of their kith and kin into slavery. Of course, the passion that this subject invokes will continue to make it a hotly-debated issue for a long time to come.

Put in proper perspective, the entire story of slavery in all of human history has been a terrible cocktail of profound ignorance, the inordinate desire of some humans to dominate their fellow humans, and sheer greed. And, just like other ignoble practices in human history – cannibalism, human sacrifice, and so on – many participated because they felt no compunction to do otherwise. After all, the general society during those dark eras in human history accepted those practices as normal.

For each era in human history, however, there have always been a noble and courageous few who harbor the kind of humane and progressive views that take our societies a few more steps towards greater civilization. The relentless campaigns of these noble and courageous few over the course of human history eventually succeeded in changing the perspectives and mindsets of their mostly obstinate fellow men and women. But for them, so many ignoble practices that have now been outlawed in modern society would linger till this day.

Without any fear of contradiction, one could say that people in the olden days perpetrated horrible crimes against humanity because they just did not know any better. Fifty to a hundred years from now, newer generations would probably frown at, and outlaw, some of the practices we find acceptable these days. Would, or should, our descendants be held guilty and accountable for those things we did because we knew no better?

My first thoughts upon coming across these documents, and listening to those a couple of those old tape recordings, were that this subject has been discussed exhaustively over the years by many. However, as advanced by Thomas Parsons in his manuscript, my thoughts could not have been farther from the truth.

As stated earlier, I have taken steps to verify most of Parsons' assertions and his perspectives on the history of the slave trade in West Africa. The truth, according to Parsons, is that there are still a few facts that are either not known or not given enough emphasis and consideration in the Western world. Even without having to conduct further investigation of Parsons' claims, a lot of what he said somehow rang true.

"Who is Thomas Parsons?" you are probably asking right now. Just as many of his closest friends did many years ago, I also came to see him, mostly by courtesy of his work, as 'the Black White Man'.

Simply characterizing what I am getting ready to tell you as just another story would not be accurate. For me, this assignment has been an interesting and exciting experience for a number of reasons.

In the first place, I got to know so much more of my dad than I ever did, and I can say that I am proud of the role he played in the events that you will soon read about. Secondly, I had cause to stop and ponder over pertinent issues and perspectives that still remain as relevant in our society today as they were many years ago.

In the following chapters, I have put together the memoirs (so to speak) of two different men – Thomas Parsons and my dad, Carl Fergusson Sr. – whose paths crossed in an incident that presented a few interesting and teachable lessons. Ultimately, this work represents the perspectives of different people with different social backdrops, the circumstances under which they met, and the events that followed.

To begin dad's story, starting from the next chapter, I will quote one of the more recent entries in his journal – unedited. This was one of his observations and comments, among many, on current local and global events.

CHAPTER ONE

CARL SR. - THE EARLY DAYS

Journal entry: January 20th, 2009 ... Tuesday

Barack Obama – relatively unknown Black kid in national political arena sworn in as President of the United States of America. And, with a Muslim name at that. Never gave him a snowballs chance in hell to make it. Ask many of us about forty years ago if a Black dude could become US President, our answers would have been the same: Not until the cock grows teeth. And I'm still wondering how it happened.

Junior told me it's not too difficult to figure out. Says he is brilliant, cool and level-headed. Saw that in the Presidential debates. Junior says his message of change appealed to a new world that has grown tired of same old political rhetoric, plus he used modern social technological tools to consolidate his campaign. Junior's friends say while others spoke about abilities to reach across the aisles, Barack Obama reached out and touched the youth of today and the leaders of tomorrow of America and the world. Very interesting stuff indeed. With this kind of attitude in selecting country's leadership, looks like good old US of A is headed for a future when men and women will no longer be ruled by color or flag, but under the banner of an all-wise and powerful God who made us all diverse and unique for very good reason.

Appears old world order is changing; moving in positive direction if White men were prepared to vote for a guy labeled as Black to attain the most powerful office on earth, and take lead in world affairs and other matters close to his heart. Huh. Beats me to think this development was achieved not by force, but by the maturing of mindset of millions of Americans. Never thought I would live to see the day when the whole world will be looking up to a Black dude to find a solution to major local and global problems. Isn't that something? As I always said, if you live long enough, you are bound to see and hear a lot of crap, but you will also definitely see and hear some really great stuff. This was worth being alive to hear and see.

... Stop by Bank to get cash to pay off bets it wasn't going to happen.

... Call Jermaine at Barber shop to cancel. Too much to celebrate today.

(End of entry)

Right from an early age, I over-heard my parents and many of the guests who thronged in and out of our home over the years discussing the ordeals of Black men and women during the days of slavery and in what our society used to be. While some of the stories were fascinating and inspiring, most of them filled one with indignation. How could any decent human beings have perpetrated such evil on their fellowmen?

My disgust with the evil of slavery or the trade itself was not helped by American History classes in High School and College which actually provided vivid images and accounts as proof of man's inhumanity to man. Better still, you could say that what almost every Black student saw was interpreted as the inhumanity of the White community towards the Black race. In every class the silence was palpable during those lectures; you could literally hear a pin drop. You could also see and feel the anger of the classroom full of all-Black students as sordid details of a shameful period in human history were presented for us to see.

Sometimes, I have wondered why generation after generation needs to be fed such hate-provoking and wound re-opening pictures. The way some of us saw it, it was like fanning and adding more coal or wood to the embers of a fire that was supposed to be dying out, just to ensure that it kept burning. But then, should the benefits that may be derived from history be sacrificed for political correctness? I can reason like this right now, but within my peer group in those days, we were almost certain that those history classes were part of a higher White agenda to further mess with the minds of Black youth.

Many of us were told, by most of those we looked up to, that White people could not be trusted. Why? White people, many adults in the Black community claimed, were always cooking up some grandiose plan or the other to subdue or destroy Black people either mentally or physically, or both.

Anyway, I am not proud to confess that my head was indeed messed up for a long time, unfortunately. Some of my closest buddies and I were privileged and grateful to learn new perspectives about slavery and the slave trade from 'the Black White Man'. But, by then, some of us had made many mistakes, took the wrong turns, and wasted so much time hate-mongering, to the extent that we had become no different than those men in history that we despised so very much.

During one of those lectures on the era of slavery, I managed to restrain myself from saying some really hateful things to the White teacher who responded to icy glares from a bunch of us with a snide remark. "And what might the problem be, boys?" he said smugly, "Just remember, guys. End of slavery or not, that does not make Blacks and Whites equal in any way or form. Don't be found where you're not supposed to be, and watch out for the signs. That's why you're getting some education". I was quite enraged by what I believed was implied in his statement, and I could hardly wait for class to be over. For the rest of the class, all I could think about was how best to get back at him without getting into a lot of trouble. The consequences of all the options pointed in the same direction – possible expulsion, and that would not go down well with my parents at all. So, I just held my tongue.

"You're an ignorant old fart, Mr. Calvin," a student yelled out at the top of his voice at the History teacher. Mr. Calvin spun around and asked as he walked towards us, "Which one of you said that?" We all looked at one another quizzically and back at him. Without saying a word, we all shrugged, even though some of us knew who it was.

The History teacher came up to me – I don't know why – and asked directly, "Tell me who it was that spoke, or you will be in very serious trouble, Fergusson," he said sternly and waited for a response.

He turned from me to look at one or two other students, and then back at me. "You disappoint me, Fergusson. I am positive you know who the culprit is among this lot. Your parents are not going to like it if you're placed on suspension, will they?" I told him I had no clue who had yelled. "Very well, then," he said, taking down the names of some of the students. "You and your cronies will be hearing from the Principal pretty soon," shouted Mr. Calvin as he marched off in anger. Everyone burst into laughter as the teacher walked out of sight. There were howls amidst laughter and clapping while Kareem Hamada shook my hands and thanked me for not giving him away. Some of his buddies came over and did the same, while other students were busy laughing their heads off.

Just like that, I became popular among the students; Black, White and Hispanic alike. Four of us got reprimanded by the Principal, except the culprit – Kareem. Can you believe that? Anyway, it was from the fall-out of that classroom incident that Kareem Hamada and I began a long and close friendship.

A part of Kareem's youth had been spent in the Middle East where his African American parents had worked and lived for many years. As we all grew up and moved on to College, he still travelled back and forth during the long summer holidays. We could never get Kareem to stop talking about the wild times he had with his Arab buddies, driving around in beautiful high-dollar cars, getting groomed almost every other day for the girls, and smoking 'shisha' at night with the boys before retiring in the early hours of the morning. His disillusionment and anger towards a society that was perceived to be engaged in an unrelenting oppression of blacks by whites, was surpassed only by his passion for Islam.

The older we got, however, the more radical Kareem's views became, particularly after the assassination of Reverend Dr. Martin Luther King Jr. on April 4 1968. In a way also, so did my views. Dr. King had preached a message of non-violence, as opposed to Malcolm X's message to Blacks to achieve what was theirs "by any means necessary". Why would White people assassinate the gentle Reverend Martin Luther King Jr., a man of peace, if they were really interested in development and progress for the Black community?

For many of us who had only been at the fringe of activism, it was time to jump in to fight for our future. Earlier in 1966, Huey Newton and Bobby Seale had founded the Black Panther Party for Self Defense, and the Party's objectives seemed quite laudable at the beginning. Somehow, the group's well-intended community programs were eventually overshadowed by legal problems, run-ins with law enforcement agencies, and internal division, among other allegations about the Party's activities. It did not take too long for the Black Panther Party to be discredited.

For Kareem and some others, there were special interests opposed to the welfare and advancement of Blacks in this country. Not even the peaceful and non-combative approach of MLK Jr. was spared of violence. All the signs, they claimed, suggested that it was time to try something radically different.

From about 1965 – 1967, racial riots were erupting all over the country. I feel certain that stories of what has been dubbed "the Long, Hot Summer Riots" dominated the thoughts and conversations of many households nationwide, both Black and White. A few of our friends had participated in the race riots in Augusta, Georgia in 1970, sparked off by the terrible death of a mentally disabled Black teenager, Charles Oatman, while in police custody. Going by the account of events, they were extremely lucky to have come out without getting arrested and without any injuries.

Apart from politics, though, Kareem and I had a few things in common. We both considered ourselves ladies men. While being studious, we also loved to party – particularly the Jamaican way, or any other way really.

Through College, Law School and Club affiliations, we had made a lot of friends that were like-minded to some degree or the other. So, we decided to form an organization of our own as a forum for discussion and interaction. Almost all of us had stories to share on old and new cases of racially motivated crimes against black men and women around the country, both teens and adults. They were either being killed or being sent to jail for the flimsiest of reasons. Also, it was evident that Blacks were mostly financially incapable of hiring quality attorneys to either defend them effectively, or seek redress on their behalf for wrongs done to them.

In many cases, we felt that the 'system' was 'throwing the book' at Blacks because most of the judges were racist. The sentences were no longer geared towards correction, but towards ensuring that they are kept away from society for as long as possible. One could say that sentences appeared to be aimed at depriving the Black minority of a future. In other words, the punishment almost always did not fit the crime.

In these modern times, private correctional facilities are incorporated businesses that trade on the stock market. Prison business is big business – still with Black young men and women making up the majority of the prison population. People are literally begging for large prisons to be built in their communities because it promotes local business. More so, nothing beats having inmates perform tasks that provide significant improvements to the financial portfolios of different companies, and for a pittance. Guess what? The longer the jail terms, the longer these commercial tasks are performed at slave wages. In other words, the government or business owners get work done for next to nothing for years on end. Unfortunately, our Black men and women continue to allow themselves to be shipped in to fill up all these prisons. If that was not slavery all over again, what other name would anyone call it? Yes, slavery is still going on – only in a different form.

Anyway, let me get back to the old days. Our motley crew – male and female from various professional fields – consisted of like-minded friends of different racial backgrounds. About forty percent of the twenty two members worked within the legal system. According to them, even though they had first-hand knowledge of what we were talking about, the judicial system still remained the last recourse for the underprivileged or the oppressed. If anything had to be done, they said, it would be best achieved by using the system to correct itself. Very soon it became clear that we had to move from rhetoric to action.

Many of us were united on a few particular points, among many others. One, most blacks are likely to be the target of racially motivated crimes. Two, most black men and women who are arrested for one thing or another, justifiably or not, lack adequate legal representation. As a result of the foregoing, most black suspects who lack the financial capability to hire good defense attorneys often find themselves accepting unfair plea bargains from District Attorneys who want a conviction one way or another. There was a widely-held opinion among us that, crime for crime, most white offenders got off more lightly than Blacks and Hispanics. Nonetheless, it did not come as a surprise that many in our now-multiracial group felt that we needed to rise above color and race.

Our services, they said, should be geared towards ensuring that our young men and women do not end up incarcerated merely because they were racially targeted, or because of a lack of proper legal representation. In addition to that, we were committed to the relentless pursuit of justice for victims of racially motivated crimes. That was kind of okay with me, but I couldn't help noticing that it did not go down too well with some. They did not hesitate to remind me that the entire concept, born as the original idea of a number of us Black guys and girls, was that we needed to focus on helping our Black brothers and sisters. However, I managed to persuade them to see the virtue of elevating our original concept beyond the boundaries of color and race.

Our group of 'comrades' suggested an official platform of some sort that could raise awareness and enough funds with which to embark on our mission. We decided on the incorporation of our organization as a vehicle to formally champion our cause. And, by no particular design whatso-ever, we found ourselves planning how best to be the legal watchdogs of people, youth in particular, in the immediate and larger communities in different parts of the country. And so was born MBSK Incorporated; acronym for My Brothers and Sisters Keepers.

Male and female, Atheist, Christian and Muslim, Black, White, Hispanic, Asian - we were united by our passion to make the legal system work for the less privileged just as well as it works for the privileged. It became our goal to ensure that the lives and enormous potentials of our youths do not waste away behind those grey prison bars. People should not be victimized just because of the color of their skin, or plead guilty to offences they did not commit just because it is the easiest way out of a legal battle they can ill afford. We had found something worth fighting for; we had found a cause. MBSK Incorporated could now begin its' journey towards national acclaim and recognition.

Even though teams were formed for specific tasks such as raising funds and public awareness, each one of us was still charged with the responsibility of doing whatever was necessary to ensure the success of our mission.

Through all of these though, we observed the strangest trend. There were more whites than blacks who were eager to support our cause and contribute funds and time to ensure its' success.

There were Government grants and other sources of funds, mostly from well-meaning deceased white men and women, to support such programs. The problem was that we had great difficulty gaining access to those funds. Through some of our White members, though, we eventually raised enough funds to fuel the pursuit of a good cause.

Curiously, concerted efforts to solicit support and funding from some of the rich and influential within the minority communities were met with apathy.

The few who granted us audience pledged very little and would not commit to any long term support, while a few found our endeavor laughable at best. They said it would be foolish for them to risk participation in an endeavor that would put them under the spotlight and banging heads with the government. Our mission, they said, could jeopardize all that they had worked so hard to get.

There was no doubt we were disappointed, to say the least. The degree of interest and enthusiasm to support a project that rang so close to home was lamentable. You could place and win a bet that two or three out of five of those we approached for support had a close relative incarcerated somewhere in the country. Eventually, we had to throw it open to the general public. Though the response was better, it still was not as great as we had expected either.

In the meantime, the more the reported stories of racially motivated crimes against Blacks and the seemingly unrelenting unjustifiable incarceration of our brothers and sisters, the more determined we were to move quickly to take-off and to succeed. Yes, the judicial system must do its' best to protect and not undermine law-abiding citizens and its' law-enforcement officers, but the justice system in those days was run by Whites to favor Whites. I was convinced that Lady Justice, blindfolded or not, must also have been deaf. While she might have weighed what was brought before her, it was obvious that she was either not listening to our voices crying foul, or that she could not hear us at all. The scale of justice was nowhere near balanced. However, compared to what Blacks went through back then, it gives me great pleasure to see that the hard work and sacrifices of our ancestors and leaders have not been in vain.

In our eyes, it was taking Lady Justice too long to dispense justice, but I guess she had not been blind to our suffering or deaf to our cries all along after all. There is no doubt in my mind that things can get better for Black men and women from here on, but only if we strive to consolidate our obvious gains instead of constantly scratching off the scab of old wounds. No wounds will ever heal quickly that way, if at all.

But, seeing and hearing what Black young men and women are doing to one another in these modern times, it grieves me most terribly that I cannot say that the souls of all who sacrificed so much for what they are squandering, can now rest in peace.

Several years of searching and playing private detectives to get information on potential cases, in order to ensure fair play, yielded some encouraging results but nothing ground-shaking. Most of the suspects tried to take undue advantage of our services, while some who got a second chance were back in court and in jail before one could blink. Sad to say, but some seemed to be getting exactly what they deserved and some probably too little.

Out of desperation, arising from a lack of success in raising enough funds and awareness, Kareem persuaded a few of the other members to support his move to seek financial support from sources outside the country. Apparently, large numbers of people from different parts of the world, some of them quite wealthy indeed, would do almost anything to obtain permanent residency in United States. Even under normal circumstances, many of them often do not qualify – citizens of certain countries in particular. For citizens of these blacklisted countries, we learned that even some of the wealthiest were not confident enough to apply for a visitor's visa for fear of being turned down.

Kareem had previously identified these opportunities as a way to make some good money for himself. He had gotten quite busy 'setting up' qualifying scenarios for some wealthy foreigners to take advantage of the different types of US residency programs available for investors. The way Kareem said it, these people were ready not only to let him make some good money, but ready to do him some favors. He had asked some of them for financial support for the MBSK project, and they were willing to help.

The way we understood it, all Kareem had to do was set things up in ways that would not put them in conflict with the United States government and the notoriously powerful Internal Revenue Service. All I can tell you is that his plan worked. There was an influx of substantial funds that were badly needed, and we also got very powerful patrons for support and logistics to embark on our mission. I guess you can say that this was how Kareem's back and forth trips to the Middle East, and continued contact with some of his friends, paid off for all of us.

"We got it made now, dudes. Now we can be assured of funding without all that crappy government paperwork or turning to some dimwits who want to see us crawl and beg for chicken change," said Kareem calling in from the Middle East. I could not remember Kareem being this excited over anything ever since I had known him. Even though he was calling from thousands of miles away to break the 'good news' to us, I could almost see his face glowing like a lighted Roman candle.

While the explanation seemed acceptable at the time, probably because we needed more financial muscle and the luxury of flexibility, I remember the cynical comments made by Jason Harris.

Jason was well-respected among the members as a brilliant attorney and one of the most insightful persons in the organization. He never said much but, when he did, his views were sometimes rattling. "And what might they be requiring from us in exchange for this … largesse and demonstration of allegiance?" No one responded. "History, guys … history. Do we have a Trojan horse here or what?"

We all looked at one another without saying a word, and looked back at Jason. With a half-smile on his face, he tilted his head to the right and said, "Sorry to rain on our parade, guys. I am only just asking, people, just asking. Don't get me wrong. I love Kareem but I cannot help being scared, even if it is a teeny weensy bit that he is often on the far right of … radical?"

With no response from anyone, Jason got up with arms outstretched. "Come on, people. Get your smiles on. Congratulations are in order. Let's go and find a decent joint to celebrate." Of course, we were happy that everything seemed just right and that the plan was finally coming together; everything, that is, except for the bizarre events that slowly unraveled and brought the man called Thomas Parsons into our consciousness.

If only Jason Harris, and the rest of us including Jason himself, knew how right he had been about Kareem having the potential to be on the far side of radical.

Within the MBSK organization, Kareem had developed a closely-knit relationship with two other members – Ali

Johnson and Mo Harvey. As we later discovered, these three had already come to the conclusion that the White-dominated system had resolved to protect its' 'own' at the expense of other "less-valuable" members of this country. Therefore, as far as they were concerned, seeking justice from the White system for crimes against Blacks was an exercise in futility. The trio of Kareem, Johnson and Harvey took it upon themselves to look for other ways to get back at those responsible for various reprehensible offences against Blacks.

To these 'radicals', as they were jokingly referred to, there was a need to have an alternative should the system fail to punish crimes against blacks, or other minorities. If MBSK was unsuccessful in its pursuit of redress for victims of hate crimes and miscarriage of justice, they resolved to design and determine appropriate punishment – unofficially.

I remember a conversation I once had with Kareem, while we were still in High school, regarding the impunity with which Whites committed all sorts of crimes against Blacks. The number of incidents increased because the perpetrators almost always got away with their crimes. That was our conclusion. There had to be some other ways to get back at the perpetrators without any reprisals to the immediate Black communities, we contemplated. After all, private individuals and law-enforcement personnel or not, these people and their families live mostly ordinary lives within our communities without any form of special protection; and they were not invincible either. It became obvious much later that those thoughts had lingered and grown in Kareem's mind.

Kareem always held the opinion that any determined and well-organized group should have a 'unit' that could exact justice on those adjudged guilty – individuals and corporate entities notwithstanding – according to the group's codes. Mo Harvey and Ali Johnson bought into Kareem's idea with great zeal. None of them seemed to care whether or not we became labeled as terrorists or the Mafia; it did not matter to them one bit. They felt compelled to send a loud unequivocal message to the general community: No longer will the Black community accept the less-than-humane treatment that has been meted out to its members.

According to Kareem and his friends, as they were later quoted to have said, never again will an organization like the Ku Klux Klan be allowed to flourish in America under any guise. No individual or group, they said, should ever be allowed again to drag this country down the road of moral and spiritual bankruptcy. We were all in agreement on that point, but there was no doubt that our vision and Kareem's extremist ideas were on a collision course. This was a problem we knew we had to address sooner than later.

Extremist views or not, Kareem was a very valuable member who had added value to the organization. From a financial standpoint, he had become the lifeline of our organization – putting in some good money from his own pocket and from his friends. The only consolation we had for now was that Athiel had become Kareem's role model. We believed that would not have much difficulty curbing the mind-set of these radicals headed by Kareem. For the moment, we needed to find a mid-ground, and it was decided that I was the best person to first reach out to Kareem.

As it was with Kareem, he had an answer for everything and there was always some new trick up his sleeve. Clearly, he had made new friends who nursed even more radical ideas that made him grin from ear to ear like a kid in a candy store. Whenever Kareem was in that mischievous mode, you just couldn't get through to him – just like the first time he invited me to meet Athiel and Tanya. That meeting turned out very well, I must admit, even though I was a bit skeptical at the beginning.

From the onset, both Athiel Brownidge and Tanya Hume struck me as a very interesting couple with wide-ranging experience. Kareem, ever so likeable and generous, was like some type of magnet that attracted the most interesting characters. I break a smile every time I recall the very first time I met the couple many years ago. I had barely pulled a chair and Kareem was already telling Athiel to show me or tell me how 'that stuff' worked.

"Come on, Doc, tell Carl how you solved our problem at Joe's Place," Kareem pleaded with Athiel who just smiled, but politely declined whatever the request was. Still so excited, Kareem turns to Tanya and begs her to tell me the 'story'.

"You go ahead and tell Carl the story, Kareem. It will sound a whole lot better coming from you," suggested Tanya, smiling and sipping her drink.

"OK, I will. Even though Athiel will not admit what he did, I am sticking with what I saw. This is something that you have to see with your own eyes to believe, Carl. I can tell you right now that I have never seen anything like this in my whole messed-up life." Kareem continued, "Remember that crazy chick with the terrible brace job at Joe's place; the one who keeps yakking away and spraying our open orders with saliva?"

"Yeah, of course" I replied laughing, "your girlfriend, Juicy, the one with the saliva in the corners of her mouth who insists on serving us all the time. Did you tell Athiel and Tanya just how much she's attracted to you, Kareem, and the calamity this crush has brought upon your friends?" Kareem's excitement turned into a scowl; he never liked it when we teased him like that. I quickly apologized and told him to go on with his story.

For your information, it all started the first time we went into Joe's. A waitress came up to our table, but Kareem insisted on 'the one with the great body' that was still busy ringing up another customer's check. Somehow unoffended, the waitress informs her co-worker that a gentleman on our table wanted service only from her and no other. Kareem waved at her to acknowledge whatever message was being passed on when she saw the waitress pointing in our direction. Soon, she glided over to our table and flashed her badly-done-brace-job at Kareem and the rest of us, "Hi, I am Amanda, Joe's cousin. Nobody has ever requested specifically for my service before; I am flattered. So, let's start with your drinks order. What can I get you guys?"

Maybe we could have managed the braces, but there were two things we just couldn't handle no matter how hard we tried; the endless salivation and the fact that she wouldn't stop talking as she brought our orders. That's why we nicknamed her 'Juicy'; her mouth just couldn't stop producing saliva long enough for her to serve us and just go away. The food in Joe's was fantastic, and the price was just as good, but Juicy drove us nuts. None of Kareem's insults worked to put her off, like when he told her "Joe needs to invest some of his profits in your mouth, Amanda. Those braces do not suit you at all." Somehow, she took it as a compliment, and remarked that she didn't know Kareem cared that much about her looks. Also, maybe on some sort of instruction from Juicy, the other waitresses would refuse to serve us if she was on duty.

Our agony had become their comedic relief because they had lied to us on some occasions that Juicy was off-duty when she was actually not – just to watch us cringe while we looked towards the exit. Sure, they knew what was going on, and it served Kareem right for thinking he had to go chasing after any girl that appeared good-looking.

Truthfully speaking, though, Juicy did seem to be on duty all the time – like her whole life started and ended in that little café. Can you imagine having to peek through, or pass by, the window of your favorite restaurant a few times just to be sure that a particular waitress was not on duty? It was stressful indeed, particularly when you were really hungry and your wallet was too thin to afford Joe's kind of good food anywhere else.

Okay, hold on for just a minute. I have a confession to make before you start wondering why we didn't just go to other nice places to eat. I had fallen head-over-heels in love with the younger sister of Anita, one of the other waitresses. From the first time I saw So-so, I knew I wanted her to be a part of my life forever. The family was from New Orleans, Louisiana, and she had come to spend some time with Anita during that particular summer. So-so was half this, one quarter that, one-eight something form over yonder, one third something else from down under, but all making up one whole beautiful angelic human being. We must all have been out of our minds to think that Pam "Foxy" Grier was the finest female ever. So-so also turned out to be as angelic at heart as she was on the outside. There is no doubt in my mind that Joe must have noticed an increase in revenue from his restaurant that summer of all summers.

You could just see all the guys, including me, with our tongues hanging out. Kareem was the first to dive in for a hook up, and we all thought it was over. Without putting too much effort, girls just seemed to go crazy for him. But, thank you Lord, not on that occasion. So-so politely requested that he should bring his friend – me – over to where they were seated. Kareem could not believe what was happening, and neither could I.

From the moment we started seeing each other, I knew my playboy days were over. For me, So-so was 'every woman' – all the women I ever dreamt of, or ever wanted. The game was over for me. I proposed a few months later, and we were married before the year was over. Like my mother used to say, "don't ever mess with a good thing." I guess now you can understand why it was stressful not being able to get into Joe's to speak with Anita after So-so went back to New Orleans.

"Juicy actually stopped talking and refused to serve us, Carl. Can you believe that?" Kareem had finally blurted out what was behind his excitement. No way, I responded. "Yes, way, Carl. Now we can sit there and eat as much as we like instead of doing those take-outs. No more nasty waitress spitting all over our food. Athiel and Tanya fixed it for good. We've been back there a couple of times and – you would not believe this – she called on one of the other waitress to serve our table."

If that was true, that was indeed newsworthy. There was this particular day, Kareem said, when Tanya and Athiel were looking for a good place to eat. He confessed to them that Joe's Place had really sumptuous and inexpensive food, but he couldn't take them there for 'Juicy reasons', as most of us had come to refer to the turn-off for Joe's lovely cuisine. So, Tanya suggested that Athiel knew a few tricks that could help. A reluctant Athiel, so Kareem said, was finally convinced by his bride-to-be to try "that stuff" on the waitress.

They had all arrived at the restaurant when, almost on cue, Juicy glided over to their table when she saw Kareem, flashing a bad brace job bathed in constant salivation like something in a bad dream. After she had introduced herself and the day's menu, Athiel and Tanya returned the courtesy by also introducing themselves. Athiel complimented Juicy on her lovely figure, and asked questions about the items on the menu. While Juicy stood by the table waiting to take their orders, Athiel reportedly looked up at her and said, "By the way, you really have no reason to like that man," pointing at Kareem, "because he always has something very uncomplimentary to say about you. You deserve the attention of other better-behaved customers who really appreciate you for who you are, and the fantastic service they get from you."

Kareem said he was ready to take off like a bat out of hell at the slightest hint that knives and glass were going to start flying through the air. Surprisingly, Juicy's only reaction was to walk away with the excuse that she had something she needed to attend to most urgently. She called on another waitress to serve them that day, and had refused to serve Kareem or any party he came with to Joe's ever since.

"Incredible. How did you do that?" I said, turning to Athiel and Tanya for an answer. Both of them smiled and Athiel insisted that he simply told her the truth. Kareem said it was more than that, but we did not have enough time to debate what happened any further because I was running late for a meeting already.

CHAPTER TWO
NOT GUILTY

O ur new organization became feverishly excited and curious when news first reached us about the subject of some public lectures by a guy nobody ever heard of before then. The lectures, we were told, were aimed at generating debate and publicity about a book, 'Not Guilty', which he was getting ready to publish. The author of the proposed book was a guy named Thomas Parsons. The news was that Thomas Parsons was anti-affirmative action, anti-reparations, and that his proposed book provided justification for the slave trade. Worse still, we were told that it contained views considered disparaging to the memory of our Black heroes. Apparently, Parsons had only recently started the promotional 'tour' of his upcoming book, and we learnt it was getting quite a bit of attention. Quite naturally, it generated so much buzz within our group, and elsewhere, it was decided that a few of us – Tanya, Kareem and I – should attend an upcoming Parsons speaking event.

Tanya Hume was a stunning beauty from the beautiful Caribbean Island of Trinidad and Tobago. She had graduated and practiced as a nurse in the Caribbean before coming over to this country to seek employment and residency. Aged about thirty-three, she looked more like twenty-three, carried herself like a model on the runway, and did so seemingly without any conscious effort. Foxy as any lady can be, she was like a voodoo priestess – doing all kinds of stuff to us guys without even having to lay a finger on any one of us. What made the matter worse was that she knew the effect she had on many of us. Unfortunately, so did her boyfriend – Athiel Brownidge.

Athiel, about fifty years old, was a British-born doctor who had just taken up residence in the United States after practicing medicine for a few years in his native country of Belize. Before that, he had done quite a lot of travelling to a number of exotic and unusual places in the world – the Far East, Central and South Africa. The Non-Profit-Organization with which he worked seemed to have gone to quite elaborate extents for the sake of getting medicines and medical supplies to remote communities worldwide. A lot of what we learned about Athiel was from Tanya, since he never spoke much about himself. Athiel (the lucky devil) was engaged to be married to gorgeous Tanya, and obviously had a lot of experience under his belt. More than anything else, both shared our vision and passion.

It didn't take too long for all members of the organization to accept Tanya and Athiel. Every one of us recognized the leadership qualities in Athiel, and we admired his even temperament and wealth of experience. At one of our monthly meetings three months after Athiel joined the organization, he was unanimously elected President. Almost immediately, he started charting a more discernible direction for the organization.

Kareem and I remembered the venue of the Thomas Parsons event. It used to be one of those 'Whites only' joints for stand-up comedy acts and small bands. It was fairly well lit, and had seating for about a hundred and fifty people. The turnout was quite good, considering that the place was almost full when we got there.

However, from the time of our arrival at the venue of the book promotion event to the time we decided to leave, that lecture was certainly an experience like no other. Much later, we all agreed there was no way anyone could sit through this mulatto guy's lectures and not find his views and arguments either interesting and compelling, or simply bold and outrageous.

"Before his retirement, a seventy six-year old white former lawmaker got a great deal of negative publicity, time and time again, for expressing his very candid opinions about Black people," Parsons started. "He was labeled racist, called all kinds of names, and had rocks thrown through his windows at home and at his cars. And it all started when he asked two rather simple questions. The first question was: For how long will the White community bear the burden and guilt of slavery? The second question was: When will the Black community consider that White people have paid in full for their role and participation in the slave trade?"

The silence in the room was deafening, reminiscent of the days in High School and College during lectures on slavery and the slave trade.

"According to that old White man," he continued, "we are defending all kinds of causes and fighting different wars in foreign countries, but we choose to remain oblivious to a cold war that has been raging in this country for so many years. He was trying to draw attention to the fact that the wounds of slavery have not healed, and that our society was getting farther and farther away from addressing the situation. Politicians do not want to address the problem, he said, for fear of being politically incorrect. He tried to warn that our society is getting more and more polarized along Black and White lines and everybody is pretending not to be aware of it.

"If a white man or woman voices an opinion that is unpopular with the Black community, then he or she must be racist, just as that old white guy was labeled. On the contrary, a black man is not considered racist even if his opinion is not just unpopular or unfair, but quite offending to the White community. There is Black group this and Black organization that, all kinds of groups and organizations, and nobody seems to see anything wrong with that. Would it be okay for the Caucasian community to do the same, he asked? When, he wanted to know, will it all end so that we can unite fully to strengthen the nation that was built on the mingling of our collective sweat and blood. When, he asked, are we going to have a truly <u>United</u> States of America?

"The way things are, he was quoted at a public event, White people generally do not feel comfortable with Black people, and Black people generally do not trust or feel comfortable with White people. However, before we rush to label such a remark as racist, maybe we should be asking ourselves whether or not the statement is true or false."

There were heads nodding in agreement, people whispering to one another.

"If there is anyone who disagrees with that statement, or if there is anyone who thinks that views such as these are racist, we can examine those opinions in the question and answer session in another half an hour or so," Parsons informed his audience, packed full of mostly White guests and a sprinkling of other minorities.

"African-Americans believe that White people still owe them for slavery. It was the old man's belief that Whites cannot seem to pay African Americans enough for their participation in the slave trade and slavery. His argument was this: If every community on the face of the earth had to pay for wrongs done to other communities during the course of human history, there would be no end to the question of reparations, or the bitterness and hatred people would harbor against one another. Politics, he kept reminding us, is a game of numbers.

"The struggle for the abolishment of slavery and the slave trade succeeded only because the larger numbers of decent White men and women who voted against the enslavement of other humans prevailed over those who either approved of it or did not care one way or another. It was all a game of numbers. Slavery was ended by decent White men and women who recognized blacks as equally human, and thus fought their own kind to put an end to the inhumanity to "fellow" men and women – color notwithstanding.

"Again, it is important to remember that their efforts prevailed because the lawmakers and citizens who shared the same views were more in numbers than those who disagreed. Numbers prevailed again and again, whether it was to give Blacks the right to vote or to allow Blacks to stand for elective offices in the nation. The success of these landmark events, said the old lawmaker, demonstrates clearly that the majority of White people have always embraced the preservation of the dignity of human beings, regardless of race or color.

"At no point, he said, did the black man or woman ever have to stand alone for recognition of rights as human beings without many White men and women standing by their sides. When Blacks cried in pain, a large number of Whites also cried with them. When Blacks bled and died, there were White folks who also bled and died with them, even though they get no recognition or acknowledgement. Each time Blacks rejoiced, many Whites rejoiced also. To him, it was unfair that many black people still expect that subsequent generations of the White race must settle what they refer to as 'debt' for the enslavement of Africans. When, he wanted to know, will this debt be considered fully paid? In other words, how many generations of the White race must pay for the participation of some, definitely not all, of their ancestors in slavery and the slave trade?"

According to the old man, Parsons continued, it didn't seem to matter whether or not many of their ancestors sacrificed life, wealth and property for freedom and equality for Negro slaves and their descendants. Not at all, he said. The way the Black community wishes to see it, this and future generations of Whites are guilty, just as all of their ancestors are guilty for the enslavement of Blacks. But, he said, not all White people participated in slavery and the slave trade.

"Even if his grandparents owned slaves and were unkind to them, that still did not make him personally liable or guilty for their misdeeds, he said. It was his opinion that the same applied to others who did not personally participate in the dehumanization of Blacks at any point in history. The old loved to refer to the Holy Bible book of Ezekiel Chapter 18 which makes it clear that God will never punish the son for the sins of his father.

"However, he was particularly passionate about the fact that some notable members of his own family either lost their lives or means of livelihood on account of their outspoken support for the total liberation of black men and women. According to the White old former lawmaker, he and many in the White community, found it rather infuriating that there is a general ingratitude and under-appreciation within the Black community of the role that decent white men and women played in their struggles from bondage to freedom.

"He found it rather unfortunate that the Black community downplays the noble role of so many courageous and God-fearing Whites who sacrificed life and wherewithal to advance the cause of their Black brethren. Why, he also wanted to know, is it that only the White race is culpable for crimes perpetrated by ancestors of both races. Yes, both races. Africans – North, South, East, West and Central – have been selling their own people as far back as anyone can remember. They were capturing and trading their own brothers and sisters long before any White slave buyers appeared on the African scene.

"Guess what," said Parsons, "they are still selling their own children, brothers and sisters till today. Whether as slaves through a trade that still thrives, or through massive looting of the resources meant for the well-being of their own kinfolk, they are still selling their own brothers and sisters. But, get this, both White buyers and African sellers of slaves made great fortunes from the slave trade. By the way, as some of you probably already know, the White old man was former Congressman Daley B. Buttons – my uncle – who has since passed on. It was at his urging that I finally decided to write a book. The title given to the book, "Not Guilty", was also his idea.

"Politics aside, he used to say, there are many leaders of the Black community who know that not all White men and women are racist, or guilty of sponsoring or supporting racially-motivated crimes, in the past or in modern society. Not too long before he passed, he asked me a few questions which I put forward to you today, ladies and gentlemen.

"Former Congressman Buttons asked, "What else must a White person do not to be seen as the enemy of the Black man? Why is it that whenever a White guy tries to do something nice for a Black guy, the Black guy thinks there must be some kind of ulterior motive behind the White man's gesture? You know we are not all like that at all, Thomas. Someone once told me that our acts of kindness are nothing but attempts to pay for the crimes of our fathers against Blacks, and not pure gestures from the heart. That kind of thought is outrageous. Black people regard us with suspicion because they feel they cannot trust us. We regard them with suspicion equally because we are never sure how they will react because they still feel embittered about how some of our people treated them. If there is no trust between people who must necessarily coexist, that constitutes a very serious problem. The White race is not perfect by any means, Thomas, and the same goes for every race. More than any other race in the world, I can say that we strive harder to improve ourselves and right the wrongs of our community, while introducing more checks and balances to prevent old mistakes from being repeated. It is by the degree of dedication to that effort we must measure one another."

Parsons went on; whipping up the emotions of his mostly White crowd.

"Ladies and gentlemen, I am getting ready to say something now that some of you in the audience might find offending, but it is the truth. There is a general belief in many African nations, and I translate: Even when terrible things happen to people, those who believe in God will always find, upon closer examination, something or the other for which they can still be thankful or grateful to God. In other words, good things have been known to emerge from situations that were originally deemed bad, while bad situations could always be worse. Whichever way I have looked at the issue of the slave trade between the West and Africa, my opinion is that the good that came out of it cannot be dismissed with a sniff. In more ways than I could have imagined, Black audiences and even close friends have never been hesitant to let me know that they consider such a statement, even the thought of it, particularly offensive. They list ills and disadvantages that really cannot altogether be ignored or 'made light of' either. However, since we cannot change what has now become history, don't you think we should explore, rather than exploit, the many ways to make the best of the freedom and opportunities that came from the sacrifices of courageous men and women? It is also my belief that a whole lot more can still be gained if African Americans, and Blacks in other Western nations, do not willfully exclude themselves from participating in the affairs of Africa (in particular) and the rest of the world.

"In the first place, the Trans-Atlantic global trade and enslavement of human beings repulsed enough White people to spark off the concerted efforts that were made to bring an end to the ignoble practice of a trade and way of life that had spanned thousands of years. The efforts continue till this day. Why? Some nations or people just can't seem to stop profiteering from either enslaving or selling their fellow humans, even in this day and age. Secondly, Blacks and Whites have integrated, in ways never before imagined, to build the most powerful nation on earth. This nation belongs to all of us. What we owe one another is a duty to further develop and protect what we jointly built, nothing more."

There was uproar in the hall. We couldn't believe most of what we just heard. Tanya, Kareem and I turned around to stare at one another, while shaking our heads in disbelief that anyone would utter such statements. From reactions and comments around us, even some of the mostly Caucasian audience appeared rather shocked at the boldness of the speaker. Tanya and I literally had to hold Kareem down on his seat. According to him, someone ought "to go and beat the living daylight out of that lunatic". We finally persuaded Kareem to let us hear Parsons through; at least for the moment.

Appealing for calm and quiet from the audience, Parsons continued. "Please let me finish. I know it seems like the wrong thing to say publicly, but you will probably be more inclined to agree with me when you hear how I came to this conclusion. While it may be politically incorrect to say certain things these days, it is my belief that we often hide or avoid the truth which will help to properly address or correct some of the harmful thoughts that we harbor against one another.

"I grew up in Africa, ladies and gentlemen, and I know what I know about the continent and its peoples not from reading an Encyclopedia, watching television, or listening to the Voice of America and the BBC.

"I am sure that most of you are probably familiar with different arguments on the impact of the practice of slavery in human societies across the continents over the millennia. There was a particular perspective that I found quite inter-esting, and I pray that this is not interpreted as an attempt by me to trivialize the human misery, pain and suffering that is associated with slavery. So, probably more in jest than with any significant level of seriousness, a few scholarly buddies of mine had suggested that slave trading throughout history and across vastly divergent cultures, represented some kind of forced emigration. It compelled the essential integration that the human family requires for real growth. Cultivating the strength and enormous potential of our diversity, they argued, is essential for humankind to realize and achieve its' greatest potentials. History, they concluded, has shown that learning to co-exist peacefully, in spite of diversity, devel-ops and shapes the soul and strengthens character. There is no doubt in my mind that humankind was created diverse for very good reason. I also have no doubt whatsoever that all races and creeds were meant by God to integrate, unite and find strength in our commonality. The questions are multifold: Did we have to resort to enslaving one another to achieve "growth and development"? How have we grown, if we have indeed grown at all, and how have the forced integration of cultures and traditions shaped us?

"Nonetheless, as educated men and women all over the world have all come to appreciate, not one nation or one people have everything that will be needed to take its people to the zenith of their potential. To do so, different peoples and cultures must cooperate, interact and share with one another, thus actuating and fulfilling the greater purpose behind human diversity.

"Has the strength of diversity not contributed to making the United States of America the most powerful nation in the world? Whether through the slave trade or emigration, people from all nations throughout the world have unwittingly made this country the capital of the world. All nations on earth have representation in America. Are we all not benefitting from the collective knowledge and skills with which humans of all races, color and creed have been endowed? While the interest in Africa might have been kindled by both its human and natural resources, I cannot help wondering where Africa would be today within the context of development, were it not for Western involvement or influence?"

Parsons spoke about the general poverty and lack of progress for blacks in many African nations till present times despite Western influence. He spoke of the lack of accountability and personal enrichment by leaders who see no wrong in further impoverishing their own kith and kin. He wondered if the Western world would ever have paid attention, as they do now, to the deplorable plight and poverty in most parts of Africa were it not for the fact that Black people have become an integral part of Western culture and communities.

Throughout history, he continued, the global human community has had to pay a steep price for progress. In a world where time can literally stand still because most cultures would rather stick doggedly to ancient traditions and superstitions, it has taken acts of war or the demonstration of superior power to shake people out of their comfort zones. At the end of it all, and without trying to justify the brutality and inhumane acts of some of our ancestors all over the globe, progress has been achieved wherever communities have allowed old wounds to heal. It is by learning to overcome our differences and living together as one that humankind can truly address itself as higher animals indeed. Slowly, but surely, humankind is moving towards complete global desegregation – an essential ingredient for global civilization.

By this time Kareem had heard enough and was getting increasingly restless. He begged us to let him leave before he hurt somebody (and we all knew to whom he was referring). Tanya pleaded with him to stay a little while longer just in case Parsons said something uncomplimentary about her hero, Dr. Martin Luther King Jr. She made it clear to Kareem that would be the signal for both of them to 'jump' Parsons. A few minutes later, however, Kareem got up and stormed out of the auditorium cursing. Kareem was obviously unimpressed, and it was clear that he was – for want of a better description – 'mad as hell'. Tanya and I decided to stay till the end of the event.

According to Parsons, people need to understand that the ignorance which breeds racism, discrimination and bigotry is a general flaw in the human race – present in all colors and cultures, and is not unique to a particular race.

"Which one of us knows the color of the Devil?" he asked the audience. "Could you identify him if he walked up to you? No, I do not think so. The only thing that we know is that a number of our fellow humans are a personification of evil, and evil has no known color. It cuts across the boundaries of race, creed or religion. Goodness, on the other hand, represents a state of human decency and spiritual well-being which is also present in all races and cultures."

In Parsons' opinion, those within whom racism and other prejudices towards their fellow humans have taken solid and immovable roots can, at best, be described as ignorant and profoundly insecure. These traits, he went on, are not unlike those exhibited by lower animals who feel comfortable only with their kind – the reason behind their natural disposition to segregation. Thus, like lower animals still, they are threatened or frightened by what they know little or nothing about.

"Regardless of how people wish to describe me," Parsons rounded up the event, "I know that I am neither Black nor White. My father was a white man and my mother was a black woman, but both of them are in me and I am proud of that. The love and strength that defined the relationship between my parents, carried and saw me through many difficult times and places. I am an embodiment of that love and strength, and the cultures and traditions both of them represent. You see, this world needs more of people whose very existence represents one bridge or another across those chasms that divide the human race, and thus prevent harmony.

"When you are the product of a relationship that defies religion, race, color and other forms of discrimination, you respect and appreciate the more important things about people and life. By virtue of their birth, some people simply straddle our world and thus have a more global perspective of peoples and issues. It is this unique breed of human beings that will sooner or later populate this world, and slowly rid it of the prejudices that have caused nothing but pain and destruction for so many for too long. That is my prediction. Like it or not, it is people like me who will ultimately make this world a better place. And no, I'm not just talking about color. You know that, right? I'm talking about all those whose very being — whose ideas and lifestyles — demonstrably defies the barriers of bigotry and all forms of prejudice."

He concluded by pointing out that while religion teaches that humans were born in sin, people like him were born and raised by men and women who had the greater kind of love and courage required to overcome the prejudices that make human society evil. Despite tremendous odds, he said, parents like his stepped across forbidden boundaries in the name of love. They refused to be cowed, bowed, or bound by the fears and superstitions that seem to define the human race. "When more and more people have the courage to cross those boundaries," he said, "that is the way that the human community will be moved forward into true civilization."

Tanya and I departed wondering exactly how to classify Thomas Parsons. By the way, I tried to get Tanya to promise not to tell Kareem, and some of the other 'hotheads' in the group, about Parsons' response to a particular question that came up during the 'question and answer session'. Sure, she said, but Kareem had been given the entire story even before I got back to my apartment.

We gave a report to the organization at our next meeting; some were outraged while others felt that Parsons did make some good points.

For me, it was neither here nor there. I learned a few things from his perspective no doubt, but couldn't dismiss the feeling that he was arrogant and somehow self-righteous in putting forward his viewpoint. In my opinion, the entire episode was something I thought we could have overlooked. The constitution of the country allowed freedom of expression and, in most cases, it did not matter how crazy or stupid it was. There was only one thing that bothered me;

Kareem and his buddies did not contribute to the discussions.

Judging by how irate he was at the venue of the lecture and much later, it bothered me indeed that Kareem did not say a word at the meeting. After the Parsons lecture, Kareem had always said that he found it particularly disturbing that Thomas Parsons, or any person who had Black blood running through his or her veins, would serve as an amplifier of the actual thoughts of Whites about Blacks. These were views and thoughts, he said, that Whites dared not or would not express publicly for fears of a serious backlash.

When the meeting was over, he got up, gave his buddies (Mo Harvey and Ali Johnson) a head signal and they all left; no smiles, nothing. Knowing Kareem for as long as I did, this smelled like trouble, big time trouble. And, boy oh boy, did we find out sooner than later how big the trouble was.

CHAPTER THREE

THE BLACK WHITE MAN

During the 'question and answer session', many issues were raised and the answers were interesting, to say the least. However, there was this one question that drew an answer from Parsons that many would not even dare think, for fear of being overheard. I will get to that in a while, after I have told you about the man some called the 'Black White Man' – real name, Thomas Parsons.

We later learned that the 'Black White Man' was a nickname given by very close friends. He turned out to be one of the most interesting men that I ever had the opportunity to come across; one with whom I later interacted under what might be described as awkward circumstances at times. Thomas Parsons' uncommon perspective had a life-changing effect on me in a way that I could not possibly have imagined at the time.

Thomas Parsons was one of two male children born in the famous Bible belt of the United States of America to a Caucasian Evangelist missionary father, Terry Parsons, and a beautiful African lady, Adawi, from the northern Nigeria Fulani tribe. The Parsons' volunteered often for missions to African countries, and actually lived in some of those countries for different lengths of time. It came to pass that one of those missionary trips required the relocation of the entire family to Africa for a number of years. And so, two years after he was born, the entire family was on its way to Africa to preach and teach Christianity to small and large communities yearning for the word of God as represented by Christianity.

It was on that trip that both he and his older brother, along with some other children in one of the villages, got infected with typhoid fever from drinking contaminated water. Sadly, the older of the Parsons' siblings succumbed to the illness. Terry Parsons' loss of his son only seemed to strengthen his resolve to seek help back in the USA to prevent more children from dying from the dreaded disease back in Africa.

Thomas Parsons survived the disease, as well as many bouts of malaria fever. "By the way, I hope you know that I am more African than all of you combined," he was reported to have been so proud to proclaim at various times during his ordeal.

At the time, under strict guidelines, churches and religious organizations were allowed to participate along with federal and state governments in providing education at all levels of society. He was enrolled in the same school system operated by the Church in which his father was a Reverend gentleman. Sadly, Reverend Parsons died on one of his missions when Thomas was about nineteen years old.

"Hey, Parsons, I guess it must be because you're bi-racial, but I hear you've got quite a story on why your friends call you the 'Black white Man'," I remarked during one of our conversations. He managed a smile and answered, "I guess you could say that. It's all in the manuscript, Carl, you lazy son-of-a-gun. Go and read the copy I gave you." I reminded him I had already gone through the manuscript twice.

The following narrative in the manuscript of his new book, 'Not Guilty', sheds light on his rather colorful background:

"...Many times I have listened, sometimes with envy, to the fun stories of family, friends and colleagues who grew up in this country. They all talk about days at the parks with family and friends, beautiful toys, their first bikes, Christmas, Halloween and Thanksgiving holidays. They reminisce about sports and pranks they played from their elementary school days to middle school and high school and college, and the schoolmates with whom they had all this fun. Most of these friends are either still around in the same cities where they all grew up, or in another city somewhere within the United States.

With me, growing up in Africa was different. Depending on where my parents were posted – town, city or village – we had the opportunity to either interact with main-stream society or the majority who lived in abject poverty.

Thanksgiving, as we know it in the United States, had a totally different meaning to thanksgiving in many parts of Africa. Thanksgiving was celebrated in churches and mosques once a week; Sundays for Christians and Fridays for Moslems during their hours of worship. When I look back, I can understand why they had thanksgiving every week. It was difficult enough making it through every single day without the basic amenities that most people in the Western world take for granted. And, if you add the fact there was little or no government support or welfare, you would certainly be grateful to God whenever you could wake up to behold another day of …hope?

I had a nice bike, which was sometimes shared with entire small communities. Even though it sometimes took a while for another turn at riding to come along, I admit that there was some gratification seeing how many smiles you put on your friend's faces. It did feel good to be the 'local champion' particularly when adult and children alike waved and called your name as you walked through the neighborhood because they had all come to see and listen to the stereo 'record changer' in action, belting out Nat King Cole, Buddy Holly and Elvis Presley tunes the night before.

At Christmas, the children got treated to different types of candy and gifts of shoes and clothes donated by the Churches. I still remember their fascination with the decorations and lights on the Christmas tree which sometimes was the only one in the neighborhood, depending on whether we were in remote villages or towns or cities when Christmas came around. Compared to their relatively simple lives, they did not miss any of these things; they were only interested in learning and broadening their horizon.

I cannot remember how many times I got into trouble with my parents for not wearing shoes or slippers whenever I was out playing with the other kids. He often remarked that the sole of my feet felt more like pure leather instead of skin. I still have not-so-fond memories of him having to pull out thorns from the soles of my feet from going hunting without footwear. What he did not understand, and maybe he did, was that shoes and slippers often made me the odd one out. As if my skin color and lifestyle were not enough, I always felt over-dressed among a bunch of my friends who sometimes did not even have shoes or clothes that had no holes in them.

On a number of occasions, mum and dad caught me in clothing that I had ripped on purpose just so that I would not look too different from the other kids. The boys taught me all sorts of interesting things; including how to make sling shots, which they called 'catapults', with which we went bird, snake and rodent hunting.

For target practice, we used lizards that were either lazing in the warmth of the tropical sun or running up walls, palm trees or any other trees. I have very painful memories of nearly blowing my thumb away from sticking it up in the path of the stone pebbles which represented the 'ammunition' for our home-made sling shots. Eventually, my skills improved. Now I feel so bad for all those poor lizards and innocent little birds that we killed. Except for the lizards, the boys cooked or roasted our kills, which included birds, snakes and rodents. Not that I needed to eat all that stuff to survive, but I have drawn consolation over the years that we killed the animals for food and probably needed a fast moving pest like the lizard for practice.

At the same time, almost all the kids were always growing or raising something; growing black-eyed beans, maize, all sorts of vegetables and tubers or raising chickens, ducks, rabbits and all sorts of small animals as pets. I raised some chickens too, and my dad encouraged me to start a garden where I grew maize, black-eyed beans, yams and sweet potatoes. Not that I ever grew enough for the family to eat, but harvest time was always so fulfilling because I saw the results of planting, nurturing and reaping.

Unlike kids in the West who had baseball, ice-skating, basketball, swimming, movies and formal music lessons for leisure, the children I grew up with had fun their own way. Tree climbing became a competitive sport to see who could climb highest and fastest, or see who could get down the quickest. Thus, it became an art that we strove to perfect. We swam in little rivers and creeks where there were no swimming pools, watched old movies projected on screens in the village or town squares whenever the occasion arose, hunted or played soccer in the daylight and wrestled in the moonlight.

We made our own musical instruments. Our flutes were made from the stalks of papaya leaves or bamboo shoots, drums from cow or goat skin pulled tight over hollowed tree trunks, and percussions from discarded milk tins or sticks and stones. In the real sense of the words, we indeed made our own music.

My childhood buddies in Africa had this great ability to fashion something interesting from almost anything available for pastime games. For instance, they would go to local bicycle repairers to get and straighten out old bicycle rims with rocks. Following that, we would cut and gather straight but rather flexible stems from particular trees to use as guides along the groove of the bicycle rims as we race around in open fields or on dirt roads. In the alternative, they would collect old tires which we slapped into motion and guided with our bare palms in races out in the fields and on anything that looked like a road within the neighborhood.

During the seasons, we climbed trees to gather fresh almonds, avocadoes, papaya, oranges and mangoes or other fruits. It was fun eating the fleshy part of the almond fruit, cracking the inner hard shell between two rocks and enjoying the juicy seed within. You know, it seemed like we ate all kinds of stuff and hardly got sick. Somehow, the food we ate was more natural and healthier than what many of us eat these days. The only problems we had to worry about were malaria and other water-borne diseases.

For many of these diseases, there were local cures from roots and herbs but there was just one serious problem.

Mum and dad said that chances were high that while the concoctions might cure the ailment, many still die from the over-dosage that eventually results in major complications.

And, many of my little friends did die too. They lost their lives to avoidable diseases which are now uncommon in the Western world; tetanus, dysentery, or malaria, typhoid and yellow fevers, among others. Childhood friends whose ever-smiling faces I still remember; whose warm embraces whenever our side scored a goal playing soccer, racing or wrestling I can still feel. These were little boys and girls whose nations are so abundantly blessed that they need not want for generations to come. Many are still being failed by the heartless crooks they call leaders in many parts of Africa, who steal and squander the resources of their graciously endowed nations.

I still have a vivid recollection of the time my brother and I got very sick from typhoid fever. Thank God I made it through. I only wish my brother had been as fortunate. That was a very painful period for everyone – me, in particular. We were very close. Well, that is life, I guess.

I must tell you about this crazy thing we used to do sometimes when we got plain bored. I think back and figure we must actually have been looking for some adrenaline rush. Anyway, we would go looking, and asking other friends, which houses within the neighborhood had the meanest dogs. The meaner and bigger the dog was, the better. We always went in search of dogs with the meanest reputations.

You could say that we just would not let sleeping dogs lie; we teased them, threw stuff at them, and called them nasty names (as if we expected them to understand us), until they got so mad they could taste our butts long before they got a chance to sink their teeth into them.

We would scramble for higher ground or run up the nearest trees for safety, or just keep running in the hope that you are faster, and have more stamina, than the dogs. Most of the time we all made it to safety, but sometimes someone would not be so lucky. A number of times we had to risk our own safety to distract the dogs in order to save our screaming buddies. On some occasions, we came across a few crazy dogs that were ready to wait patiently at the bottom of the tree for your butt to get down. I can remember a few of us trapped up some trees for upwards of an hour, maybe more. What kind of mongrels were those, I often wondered. Anyway, at no time did any of those mongrels ever get me, just in case you were wondering. That was because I had proven myself to be the fastest of the bunch time and time again, even if I say so myself.

Looking back now, High School, or Secondary School as it was called, was also so much fun with friends from extremely diverse backgrounds, all those teachers and their funny nicknames, and our numerous escapades. There was the teacher and House (dormitory) master that was nicknamed 'Mango' by the students because his head was shaped like a mango; really. Then there was the young and very attractive female French teacher who made us daydream through all her lessons. Very few students in our 'boys only' boarding school paid very little attention in class to ever understand the French language. Too many of us were totally messed up in French for life. Thank goodness Chinese is now a more preferred language for business these days.

It was a boarding facility with about six hundred students. It was the equivalent of combining Middle School with High School. The experience was great and it really was so much fun once you got through the early years. Parents were nowhere near, and visiting days were once every month. You could obtain special permission – an exeat – if there was an urgent need to go home before 'open or visiting day', of course. Other than that, you were literally on your own, far from where your mother could hear you crying from some serious butt-whooping.

The boys were nicknamed after some of the most embarrassing or memorable incidents in the early years of their High School life, the sports they played either so well or so badly, the food they loved, the way they looked and so on. These nicknames sometimes changed as we all grew up; better or worse. We sneaked out many times to watch movies or visit night clubs that were in 'forbidden territories'.

Among so many pleasant and not-so-pleasant memories, I recall very clearly the strange but interesting fact that there was no running water almost all the time. For a kid who travelled back and forth to the United States where running water was a given, it was hard for me to understand why running water in many parts of Africa has to be a luxury. The list of requirements for boarding accommodation included a bucket, and it did not take too long for you to find out why. We all had to store water in buckets, one way or another.

Water was delivered in a five hundred gallon water truck to the entire school population only two to three times a week. Sometimes we barely had enough to fill a cup to brush our teeth or wash the toothbrushes. There were no showers, so you had to dip little bowls in the bucket to pour water slowly over the body to clean away soap lather. If you were not lucky enough to get water from the school central tank after staying in long lines for hours, you had one other alternative. You would have to wake up in the very early hours of the morning to walk about half a mile to get water from any of the few ponds in the area before they got muddy from excess activity. I remember this in particular because I could never get used to the pond water despite the disinfectants that we brought to school as part of the 'survival kit'. Some of us always broke out in terrible rashes. It was very hard, but we all got through it somehow.

On other more dignified occasions, we had the pleasure of strolling down 'Lovers Lane' (as we called the road leading from our campus to the all-girls High School adjacent to us). This was possible only on those far-in-between evenings or nights when there were High School Theater or School Band performances, Inter-school debates, or sporting events among others. These special evenings provided the opportunity for us to hold hands with our 'heartthrobs', or sneak a few kisses if it was dark enough and their chaperons were nowhere in sight.

So, you can imagine how taking a bath was not just compulsory whenever those special events came up, it was war if you could not get any water to do so. These were moments we all longed and rehearsed for; the day newcomers to the dating game stammered and made their first move and the day others had to hone or cement their social skills. How could you possibly not have water on those much-awaited occasions? You did whatever you had to do; steal a few scoops of water or take the entire bucket if it was not secured. At that critical time, no one cared whether or not the water was from the pond.

University was no less interesting exploring newly-gained freedom. Until then, coming from my background, I could not possibly imagine how two lovers could engage in sexual intercourse in a room shared with other students. To look or not to look; that was the question. Whichever I decided to do, and believe me I did try both options, I thought I would die – and I was pleasantly surprised that I didn't. The elite fraternity to belong to was 'The Sea Dogs'. [Author's note: Co-incidentally, one of the original members and founders mentioned by Thomas Parsons is now internationally recognized and celebrated as one of the world's great literary giants.]

Initially, I wondered why my parents had to give up the comfort of Western society for the 'hard and harsh' way of life in Africa. Sometimes when those living conditions got almost unbearable, I found it very difficult to understand or appreciate my parent's decision to live and work in Africa, to say the least. But, looking back at it all, I am proud of my parents for their sacrifice to the less-privileged of our world and for the experiences I shared with them with so many wonderful people. I probably would not have minded following in the same footsteps as my parents, but for one reason. I do not see Africans as being anywhere near ready to make the kind of sacrifices that will ensure a better future for their own people.

Here in the US, it was always rather amusing when many of the friends to whom I have narrated my experiences in Africa look at me like some kind of 'modern day Tarzan'. Sometimes I get the feeling that they are envious of my out-of-the-ordinary boyhood experiences. In Africa, they call me a 'white man' while the 'white men' in the West call me a 'Black man' because of Jim Crow Laws and my upbringing. I guess that's why many in Africa refer to me as the 'Black White man'; a nickname I did not take kindly to at first.

It was as if I was one color on the inside and another on the outside. So, I guess one could say that I was either color-less or colorful; that is, of course from a personal perspective which depended on my mood on that particular day.

Living in a world where acceptance and recognition are strictly limited by one color or the other – nothing in-between – was not easy for me growing up. There are very few people who know this, but there were so many times that I wanted to be either so 'Black' or so 'White' that it hurt. Look at me. I was raised in Africa by a Black mother, but I am of a different skin-tone because my father was

White. I am bi-racial. White people do not regard me as White because of my Black mother, and Blacks have told me that I could never understand what it means to be Black even if I was born by an African woman and raised in Africa.

Both Blacks and Whites question my identity and loyalty because our 'xenophobic' societies consider race and color as critical in determining who you really are and where you really belong. You are considered an outcast by every community if you do not fit into their specific strait-jacketed definitions of "our kind". Too many times, I wanted to really belong somewhere – with one's own kind – in a community where you imagined you were welcome and appreciated. Even though there are a lot of multi-racial people like me in different parts of the world today, we do not have anything that resembles a 'community', so to speak, to interact and share experiences.

Growing up to see how limited in thought and imagination most human beings can be, I have always admired and saluted the courage of parents like mine. My parents, and many like them all over the world, transcended physical and psychological boundaries that were erected, out of fear and insecurity of the unknown, from ancient times. For love and with an abundance of courage, they rose above and beyond the small-mindedness of their societies to embrace the world. They saw no color. They saw people of all races and backgrounds purely as fellow human beings.

Although perceived by many in olden and current times as traitors and a disappointment to their families and communities, I am convinced that all those who were brave enough to challenge ancient unprogressive traditions will one day be seen as heroes. That is, heroes who helped the human spirit soar to a new and greater level of awareness and maturity.

While these boundaries may have been excusable when humankind lacked a global knowledge of the diversity of our world, there is no reason why such boundaries should still be relevant considering what we now know. Science has proven that all humans have more in common than not. Yet, most people are still very uncomfortable when confronted with the reality of a changing world whose walls are beginning to collapse, and whose boundaries are becoming blurred.

Eventually, at the end of a long inner struggle, I found the confidence to believe in myself. I strode across continents with courage. After all, I represented an embodiment of diverse cultures; an embodiment of national flags. I could see the beauty of our world in its full colors just as God sees it. I could understand the uniqueness of the single and the beauty of the whole, and I had finally found peace within my soul to be able to face the world without fear."

When it came to the question and answer session at the Thomas Parsons book promotion event, Tanya and I had become very curious to find out what kind of questions would or could be asked, and what kind of answers the 'crazy' Parsons would offer. Were we disappointed? No. On the contrary, we were flabbergasted, particularly by his answer to a question regarding a comment attributed to Late Congressman Buttons.

It had started off nicely with someone in the audience asking about the issue of reparations for African American descendants of slaves.

Parsons asked why it should be an issue at all. So, he asked, why are reparations required only from the White nations that traded in slaves, and not from the now oil-rich African nations that sold and supplied slaves willingly? He said that he really did not want to get involved in those rather tiresome 'for and against' arguments about how to calculate cost, which nation or private institutions or individuals benefitted, and direct payment or no payment to individuals or groups. Neither, he said, would he argue with those who support the view that the Western powers at the time, including our dear nation, accumulated a great deal of wealth by the use of Black slave labor. There are a lot of fundamental issues yet to be addressed regarding how "business" is conducted by Western nations in Africa.

Unlike trade between Western nations, rules do not exist to ensure that both buyers and sellers of natural resources do not engage in plundering, exploitation and corruption of host nations and peoples. When slavery and the slave trade came to an official end, unscrupulous Western businessmen and their local cohorts developed new strategies to ensure continuity for their mutually profitable evil ventures. Both sides of the trading spectrum invested heavily in the promotion of poverty and chaos to ensure two main goals.

The first goal was to ensure perpetual continual discord, thereby making it inherently difficult for African communities to find the peace and unity that are required to develop viable economies on which to build stronger communities. The second goal, creating poverty even in the midst of abundance, ensures that the people's bellies are not filled enough to enable rational thinking. Generally speaking, constant attempts seem to be made by both African and foreign unscrupulous business interests that are calculated to keep the average African thinking only of just how to survive each grueling day on earth.

Parsons lauded the spirit behind affirmative action when asked for his opinion on the subject which was first introduced in an Executive Order (10925) signed by President John F. Kennedy in 1961. The measures, to achieve non-discrimination, were first modified in 1965 by President Lyndon B. Johnson to ensure that Federal contractors hire without regard to race, religion and national origin. It was modified again in 1968 to include gender, a move described by Parsons as long overdue.

Yes, he said, there is justification for affirmative action – in that it is meant to compensate for past discrimination, persecution by the ruling class, and to address existing discrimination. However, he continued, it is important to ensure that it is used to provide what it was intended for – equal opportunity, and not to promote the lowering of standards for Blacks.

"Time and time again, Black men and women have demonstrated equal or better capacity when compared to their peers from any race or of any skin color, in every field of endeavor whenever given the opportunity of a level playing ground by the government. While many who are financially incapable of getting a good formal education might indeed need help to achieve success in their aspirations, 'affirmative action' will not change how growing competition in businesses worldwide interprets the word 'qualified'.

"It's a good thing to try and find ways of creating opportunities for the under-privileged to get a shot at success in life, but our society must work towards creating an environment where 'affirmative action' will no longer be necessary to ensure that people are judged by merit, and not by gender, religion, or the color of their skin. Affirmative action still represents discrimination in some form. Whichever way you slice it, discrimination is discrimination.

"In some parts of the third world, where it is referred to as the 'quota system for the underprivileged', it not only slowed down the nations' progress, but literally destroyed any progress that had been previously achieved.

"Also, with the exception of games like ice hockey or events at the winter Olympics, it is a known fact that major sports are dominated by Blacks. I do not think I need to tell you that these Black sports superstars did not need 'affirmative action' to qualify over many other Whites who also vied for those enormous revenue-generating positions. Many Black people have demonstrated that they can work as hard as anyone to achieve the required academic excellence and qualifications for survival in a competitive job market. And, just as some Blacks have qualified for coveted positions in national sports, the field of entertainment, and other industries, more of them can do the same as long as they are not unjustly denied the opportunity to try. As notable Black leaders like Frederick Douglass implied in their comments, it is insulting that anyone should suggest a lowering of standards to enable the participation of Black people in any field of endeavor."

Then, a bespectacled Black dude who identified himself as Sidney, sporting a short Afro hair-do and wearing a black leather jacket raised his hand to be allowed to speak. He was granted permission by Parsons to go ahead.

This dude took everyone down memory lane to make his point. He recalled the fact that sometime in the seventeenth century, about 1667 according to some records, the Dutch colonial masters freed a number of slaves to whom they gave properties in what is modern day Manhattan (New York).

These slaves, he said, had their properties taken away from them by British colonial masters who forbade property ownership by Blacks in 1712, thus depriving these Black families what had rightfully become their own, and without any form of consolation whatsoever. In some major cities in the South and in the North, the dude who identified himself as Sidney continued, there were freed slaves before and after the creation of this country in 1788. By a familiar White "miracle", however, Black men and women and children who once were free found themselves enslaved all over again.

Sidney wasn't finished: Just after the American Civil War and the Reconstruction Era, all the rights that Blacks had fought so hard to get were once again taken away from them, most particularly in the South. The success that had been achieved through the efforts of some Black heroes like Harriet Tubman and Frederick Douglass were taken from us just like that — once again. Black people in this country became gradually enslaved again; that is, enslaved and brutally treated for more than sixty years until the emergence of the African-American Civil Rights Movement in 1954. Slowly, but with great sacrifice and many casualties, the Black community fought to regain our freedom and self-respect. We continue to be engaged in what seems like an unending battle merely to ensure a better place in this country for ourselves and our children.

Parsons shook his head and said emphatically, "Great sacrifice and casualties that included many Whites and other minority groups that sympathized with the Black cause. As always, you are downplaying the fact that Black people did not achieve success alone. It is a known fact that many men and women of other races, fought and died with the Black heroes that are acknowledged in Black history. Black people hardly ever give Whites and others credit for anything. That is what makes me so mad."

Sidney, the Black dude, retorted spontaneously, "Are you aware of the fact that African-Americans have fought and shed blood in every war or cause in this country, including the War of Independence, side by side with those they thought to be their White brethren? Can you give me one reason why your White folks downplay the fact that they did not achieve success alone either? Why do they downplay the fact that many Black people marched, fought and died with them? What manner of people, except for a greedy and God-less one, would climb on your back to gain wealth and power, and then turn around to use that same wealth and power as tools to oppress and dehumanize you? Must Black people always have to beg to be treated fairly and given an opportunity to eat from the fruits of their labor? That, Thomas Parsons, is what makes me harbor resentment and distrust for the White man."

Parsons asked, "Have you given some thought to the fact that people of different races and cultures probably have cause to bear various degrees of resentment towards one another for past ignoble acts? There is a lesson to be learnt in how they suppress feelings of hate or resentment to work together for the common good and progress of the global human family."

"It used to bother me, but not anymore. A lot of White folks still harbor residual racism which always seems to rise to the surface when confronted with assertiveness from individuals who, not too long ago, could not drink, sit or eat with them in the same place. Perhaps they expect Blacks to grovel eternally to show how grateful we are for being recognized as human, after all?" Sidney interjected.

"Not grovel," Parsons responded, "but perhaps you should not lump the good ones with the bad ones. That way, maybe the descendants of those who helped and died for you will not see you collectively as a bunch of ingrates. They are human too, you know; expecting just a little acknowledgement for those of their ancestors who provided light and hope during periods of darkness and fear. But, have you stopped to consider why Blacks in Africa generally do not harbor as much anger and resentment towards Whites as do Black descendants of slaves in America and elsewhere in the West? It's because their understanding of the history of slavery and the slave trade is significantly different from yours.

"Let us consider four facts. One, not all slaves in the history of the African slave trade were taken outside Africa. Two, the dehumanization of the slave was greater in Africa than it was in the West. Three, slave traders in the West were more eager to put an end to slavery than their counterparts in Africa. The fourth fact is that there are also descendants of slaves in different parts of Africa; that is, the descendants of slaves who were sold to other warlords and other tribes within the African continent. So, how come Africans, descendants of slaves or not, generally do not harbor the kind of residual anger or resentment towards White people as do descendants of slaves in the West?"

"And what exactly is your point, sir?" asked Sidney.

"I have observed that a lot of Blacks in this country harbor so much anger towards Whites only because they are seen as the race that has always exploited and victimized Blacks. The way I see it, the Black race has been more a victim of their own nature than a victim of the White race or any other race. The truth is that Black people have always been their own worst enemies, and therefore victims of their own people more than any others."

"You spoke about residual anger. I say to you that any residual anger within the Black man is justified, particularly when it is agitated again and again by residual racism — manifesting in blatant injustice and ongoing discrimination that threatens to destroy everything that Blacks have worked so hard to achieve. And then, there are people like you who always attempt to understate the indescribable mental and physical suffering of African-Americans under slavery and through the 'Jim Crow" era; the consequences of which can still be seen and felt in current times." The Black dude concluded, gathered up some documents and walked away from the event while a number of people were still clapping for him.

"To some extent, the gentleman's comments are true, but we all need to find a way to get along", Parsons said to his audience. "Come on, guys. There's a reason the windshield is bigger than the rear-view mirror. While it is okay to glance occasionally in the rear-view mirror to see what you are leaving behind, it is more important to maintain a focus on the larger windshield through which you can see the bigger picture that lies ahead. Plus, you could run yourself and others off the road if you are perpetually gazing into the rear-view mirror, instead of focusing on the journey forward. For me, it's about where we go from here, more than where we were yesterday."

Then an older Black guy, who said he worked as a journalist for a local Black publication, raised his hand and was allowed to speak. "Is there any truth to stories that your deceased Uncle, former Congressman Buttons, once said that Whites are a better people than Blacks?" It was clear from the way he asked the question, notepad and pen in hand, that he was daring Parsons to answer a question to which he already knew the answer.

"That is true," Parsons replied, making no effort to avoid the cold gaze of the guy who had asked the question. "He did say that on a few occasions, though in private conversations with those he considered friends. As he came to know later, some of those friends had shared what was supposed to have been a private conversation with members of the public."

Amidst the murmuring, the Black journalist could be heard trying to follow up on his question with little success. Parsons made a motion with his hands to appeal to the audience for some quiet so that he could hear what the guy was trying to say.

"Did he share with you the basis for such a racist view and remark," the man continued, "and do you share the same views, by any chance?"

"Yes. That would be the answer to your questions. Also, in my opinion, while such remarks may be considered arrogant,

I do not believe they were racist," Parsons responded. "The Jews say that they are the chosen people of God – favored and considered to be more significant than any other humans on the planet – and no church-goers, Black or White, seem to have any problem with their claims. Congressman Buttons made those remarks based on what he had observed within Black communities in this country and in Africa."

You could barely hear Parsons say "And I will tell you why" because of the uproar. A few people got up and left, while some others could be seen preparing to leave at the drop of a hat in case the ongoing hullabaloo turned even uglier. The speaker appealed for calm, while he got ready to speak. Almost immediately, the little hall became so quiet you could hear yourself breathing.

"The Late Congressman came to the conclusion, and I fully agree with him, that there is probably only one major difference between White people and Black people. Although most people labeled him racist, his opinion had nothing to do with color. If anyone asked him for one word to describe the average Black man, he said that his response would be – selfish. And, for the average White man, the word he would choose would be – selfless. So, after sharing notes and experiences, we were both in agreement that most Black people are selfish while most White people are selfless."

That was it. For Tanya, as well as the few minorities in the audience, that was the cue to leave, with most cursing angrily and hurling obscenities at Parsons on their way out.

He was still at the podium trying to explain his position, but we were already at the door with others who felt they had heard more than enough, expressing shock at what she described as garbage. Tanya could hardly wait to get back to the others to share all that we heard, particularly after Kareem had left.

CHAPTER FOUR

THE JOURNEY AND THE ORDEAL

The hospital room was suddenly filled with loud bleeps that left me wondering whether to run out to get help or to stay with my new friend through whatever crisis was unfolding. Even though he appeared calm outwardly, the querying look in his eyes showed that he was rather perturbed about the cause of those bleeps. My friend, Thomas Parsons, was hooked up to all kinds of machines and monitors, with tubes connected to his body and cables running under his hospital gown.

Irene, Parson's White cousin had rushed out of the room to get help from the nurses' station. She came back into the room almost immediately with two nurses. One of them went straight for the monitor to silence it, while the other nurse raised his hospital gown to reveal and adjust the clamps and leads to the Electrocardiogram machine. The nurses smiled and assured us, me in particular, that there was no problem. The nurse must have noticed me trembling. They advised, however, that I needed to wind up my visit so that Parsons could get some rest. And, that was exactly what I did. I left the room, but I did not leave the hospital until I finished reading the typed sheets of paper to which he had been trying to draw my attention when all hell seemed to break loose.

I cannot tell you why, but I never really liked hospitals. It did not matter whether I had to go there for a doctor's appointment or to visit a sick friend or relative. However, since Thomas Parsons' admission into the Intensive care Unit, I had visited him more times than I had ever been to a hospital my entire adult life. It was so sad to see him lying in that hospital room looking so fragile and sapped of that vibrant energy and optimism that never failed to inspire and infuriate his audience at the same time, and every single time. That was the effect that the Black White man had on people – you either hated or loved his bluntness, boldness and confidence. But, everything else aside, you could not deny that Thomas Parsons had the "gift of the gab".

Irene, quite pretty and much older than Thomas Parsons, was the only relative I had seen with him since he was admitted into the hospital. Going by what I was told when we were introduced, she was the only child of his father's older sister. She was married to a wealthy local newspaper publisher and had three grown children – two boys and a girl. Apart from having something very motherly about her, it was obvious she cared very deeply about her cousin.

Irene was always by Parsons' side – making sure he ate well, running some errands on his behalf, and typing his hand-written manuscripts. According to the nurses, she was always the first visitor to show up and the last to leave. They said she never talked much, but she always wore a very warm smile.

Parsons had arrived in the Emergency Room very close to death. As a matter of fact, from opinion of ER staff many hours after he came in, he was not 'out of the woods' at all. Echocardiogram and electrocardiogram tests revealed that his heart was in failure. His blood pressure was so high you could say he was getting ready to 'blow a gasket'. The results of a Holter monitor test gave a dire picture. During the twenty-four hour period monitored by the device, it was discovered that he had literally 'died' thirty-five times for periods ranging from about five to twelve seconds.

This meant that his heart stopped beating thirty-five times for those brief periods, a stage of clinical death, only to 'jump-start' itself back to life again. The doctor also said that his heart was in constant atrial fibrillation. All these translated, I was told, to complications of a heart disease for which he had been receiving treatment – dilated cardiomyop- athy. Parsons said that he had been taking a daily cocktail of powerful drugs for about two years. The current emergency was triggered off because he abruptly stopped taking his medication, and had not been able to do so for about a week.

Before the alarms went off, Parsons had been telling me about the experience that aroused his interest in the slave trade; that is, apart from what was taught under the 'History' curriculum in certain West African nations and schools.

During one of those hot and humid summers in the early 70s, Parsons recalled, he had secured a vacation job with a local construction company. It had indeed been a privilege to travel from the former capital of Nigeria, Lagos, to the construction site – the premises of government-run Administrative Staff College – in the historic beach city of Badagry.

The old historic city of Badagry, located along the coast of Nigeria, was reputed to be the largest slave-trading post in West Africa. "I could never have imagined just how profoundly that trip would slowly shape my thinking, and ultimately affect my life", he said. As the second weekend approached, one of the local staff of the company had suggested a visit to the site of relics from the slave trade era. Since there was really not much to do on a weekend in that neck of the woods, except one was interested in trying out different types of lovely seafood dishes, he said that a few of them agreed to take the trip.

After the conclusion of the official tour of what remained as very sad memories of the era of slave trading, Parsons said he took off his shoes and socks, rolled up the legs of his pants to the knees and decided to take a walk on the beach. According to him, every step he took on the little stretch of Atlantic Ocean beach seemed to land in what felt like a permanent impression of the footprints of one slave and another.

All of a sudden, he said, a huge wave approached the seashore threateningly, only to reduce in fury as it rolled in just ankle-deep. According to Parsons, "As the waters receded, the soft, white sands of the beach seemed to reveal tracks of a multitude of bold small and large footprints coming from onshore until they disappeared into the shallow waters of the Atlantic Ocean." Even though many of his buddies attributed this "experience" to a normally fertile imagination gone wild, he said that the picture remained permanently imprinted on his mind. Even after hundreds of years, he said, those footprints seemed to have been invisibly preserved as part of a silent pact with the powerful Atlantic Ocean waves that often showed no mercy as they hit, and receded from, the shores. It all seemed so eerie, he admitted.

Parsons went on, "In deep contemplation, I had tried to imagine the horrors that were described by the tour guide. He spoke somewhat dispassionately, in broken English, of the last journey of many thousands of young men and women who had been captured for sale into slavery by raiding parties of their kinsmen (not the White buyers). The guide spoke of the reported excitement of local slave dealers at the appearance of the slave ships and traders, while shudders ran through even the bravest of captured slaves in the knowledge that the dreaded hour of their departure into the unknown had finally come."

The slaves, he said, were exchanged for a combination of firearms and various personal items that were strange but fascinating to the natives; guns, simple tools, mirrors, hats, shoes, alcohol, western clothes and so on. In those days in West Africa, trade was mostly by barter and the local currency was in the form of cowry shells.

"There we were, Carl" he said in a somber voice, "in the same holding areas where men held their fellow men and women captive (in anticipation of the arrival of slave-buyer clients) for the love of wealth and power. And there they still lay – the corroded shackles and the padlocks, among other relics of a then-flourishing business in the sale and exchange of humans, which held down their own brothers and sisters like animals awaiting slaughter. The combination of all those things bore witness to one of humankind's most ignoble practices."

"Hard as I tried", he continued, "I tried to imagine the fears and thoughts of those men and women, hundreds of years ago, as both sellers and buyers examined them like mere commodities. Naturally, as has been the tradition in most African countries, there would have been some haggling over price, after which the captives would be traded and handed over to their new owners.

"With all of them crammed well beyond the capacity of the dank holds of the slave vessels, they embarked on an uncomfortable and unwilling journey with total strangers into stranger worlds and situations. All those young half-naked men and women from a tropical climate must have gone through hell with the severe temperature changes of the oceans and at most of their different destinations. Even the coldest night of the dry dust-filled Harmattan season in

West Africa was never quite below fifty degrees Fahrenheit. How did they cope? Many, as we know, did not survive the long periods of starvation, the hardship of the long journeys, and the consequent depreciation of health.

"I was overcome by wave after wave of emotion as I tried to imagine what could have been on each of their minds – bound, helpless and probably wounded during capture – as each of their feet left was lifted of the shores of their motherland, to climb onto vessels bound for strange and unknown destinations. Their sad journey into the unknown started right here on these shores, and I was walking on the same ground on which those young men and women had trodden as they embarked on a journey that would change their lives and ultimately change the world."

Apparently during the slave-trading era, the coastal town of Badagry, located in Nigeria close to the boundary of the former French Colony called Republic of Benin on the shores of the Atlantic Ocean in West Africa, had been a massive thriving slave market. As a matter of fact, Badagry is reputed to be the point from where the largest numbers of slaves were transported overseas. The other point of extraction of slaves from Nigeria was through the pre-colonial Kingdom of Akwa Akpa (with the current city of Calabar as the administrative capital). Slaves extracted through the Badagry port were mostly from the Yoruba and Benin (former Mid-Western Nigeria) tribes, while slaves from the Igbo (Eastern Nigeria) tribes were transported from the Calabar port.

Although he didn't produce official data to support his claim, Parsons said that the largest percentage of all the slaves taken from Africa was of Nigerian origin. That, of course, was not difficult to believe considering the fact that Nigeria has the largest Negro population on the face of the earth.

By his reckoning, many of the slaves taken to Haiti and the Caribbean Islands originated mostly from a rich cultural Yoruba heritage in the old Western region of Nigeria. All you need do to be a believer, he said, was to compare the ancient folk and traditional art or sculptures of these communities. In Brazil, he said, there is a small population that still speaks the Nigerian Yoruba language fluently. The same tribe has kept most of the traditions, which they practice even in these modern times. Nigeria was definitely the most fertile ground for a continuous supply of healthy and able-bodied men and women, especially for the trans-Atlantic slave trade.

"Looking out from the shores towards the magnificent Atlantic Ocean," he said, "the foaming waves lost power as they rolled in around my feet. I suddenly noticed an old lady standing about five feet away from me, smiling. As I gathered later, she was known throughout the community as Granma Senami; the oldest living inhabitant of the historic slave town of Badagry and a living history of the culture and tradition of the people. While no one knew her exact age, Granma Senami was believed to be no less than a hundred years old.

"I remember seeing her in the distance seemingly combing the beachfront for shells or some other rarities. But, just before I got to where she was, I had stopped to enjoy the feeling of having salty Atlantic water splashing all over my face and body as the waves rolled in. That moment was quickly interrupted by the terrible feeling I used to get as a child of an attempt by the mighty ocean to pull me into its depths as the receding waves dragged sand away from under my feet.

"Apparently, the old lady had caught up with me while I was still absorbed in my thoughts. I didn't know how long she had been standing there, but it really didn't matter. Slightly startled at first, her gentle eyes and warm smile were reassuring. We exchanged greetings, after which she appeared to be gazing at something, or nothing, in particular across the expanse of the Atlantic Ocean. I tried to follow her gaze, but there was nothing more to see than the constantly forming waves and mass of water, the thundering sound of the Ocean, and the beautiful horizon where the ocean seemed to merge with the sky."

Parsons said that as Granma Senami gazed across the waves of the Atlantic, he could almost imagine that she was, in her mind's eye, putting together pictures and memories of a distant and exciting past. Without looking directly at him, and as if on cue, Granma Senami said, "According to our parents and great-grandparents, there was great commotion in the village when fishermen first set eyes on the outlines of something that had come from another world. They rowed quickly back ashore, while instructing all the children swimming close to the shore to get out of the water fast and run to their homes.

"Very quickly, our most renowned warriors and elders had been informed of the danger. They put on their war garbs, and armed themselves with very powerful charms and amulets and other weapons," she continued in the local language. Parsons said he initially believed that she was addressing someone else, but there was nobody else but the two of them. At the same time, he said, even though she appeared to be speaking to no one in particular, he somehow had the feeling that he was her intended audience.

If this old lady was prepared to tell him a story, Parsons said that he was certainly ready to hear it. And so, turning to face her directly and taking two short steps forward to get me close enough to her, he said that he gave her his full attention.

Granma Senami told Parsons that all the women (with the exception of the warriors among them) and children were sent to their homes or into hiding. They commandeered some of the best canoes moored on shore and rowed out to meet the danger face-to-face. That, she said, was the way of those who were referred to, and regarded, as men. They met known and unknown danger head-on. The danger, this time around, was the massive vessel in which the first set of Europeans appeared on the scene.

The local warriors, both old and young, had braced themselves for the worst until they saw human-like figures waving at them from the deck of the ships as they probably considered whether or not it was safe to drop anchor. Grandma Senami said that the warriors not only waved back, but beckoned for them to come closer. According to the stories they were told, she said, many of the strangers stayed back in the huge boats while some of them climbed into smaller boats and came ashore. The story went on to suggest that curiosity and the acclaimed warmth and hospitable nature of West Africans, more than better judgment, informed the natives' invitation of the strangely colored men ashore.

She told of how the visitors, eager to make friends, had come ashore bearing gifts of all kinds to a curious and receptive but still suspicious crowd. The many gifts included mirrors, muskets, hats and western clothing, refined sugar, whiskey and other items considered strange but interesting during the era.

According to Parsons, Granma Senami, laughing and revealing a lot of missing teeth, said their great-grandparents and other elders told them many funny stories about the strangely colored visitors. The funniest, she said, was how they reacted to mosquitoes, and how their bodies reacted to mosquito bites. Also, she said that many laughed at how they seemed to speak through their noses, their very strange clothing and the fact that they just couldn't stop sweating and changing colors.

Anyhow, Parsons said that the story went on to suggest that both parties began to relax their guard as tension and uneasiness gave way to fascination as the methods of communication improved. "Then," he said, "She turned to look at me directly and smiled stating their great-grandparents said that was how it all started. Some of them were good, she told me, and some were very bad to our people. They were of the same kind like some that we have been seeing around here in recent times, she stated, pointing out that I look a little like them."

Right before their eyes, she told Parsons, so many people were swallowed up in the big boats like magic, sailing towards where no man had ever gone and come back to tell. "They all disappeared. No one ever saw them again, and nobody has seen any of the young men and women those people took away." She paused for a few seconds and wondered aloud. "Are their children's children – our relatives – really alive and doing well in faraway strange lands as we have been told?"

Without waiting for any answer in particular, she looked straight at me and said, nodding, "Many of us had fathers, mothers, brothers, sisters and relatives who were taken from us, you know. Many of us did." I tried to assure her that the stories were true – the offspring of their relatives taken into captivity were mostly okay and doing great things in some of the greatest countries in the world.

"Dead or alive," she sighed, "we have never stopped praying for them; hoping that even if we never see them again in flesh, we will all be reunited once again in the world of dreams where spirits live and roam freely."

Parsons said he stayed back to ask more questions and got very interesting answers that were significantly different from what millions learned as part of both primary and secondary school education in some parts of West Africa. The difference, however, was actually meeting a person who was not too far removed from events that you are taught only in History classrooms.

"Incredible story," I told Parsons when I went back into the room to check on him on my way out of the hospital. He was awake, and one of the nurses was in the room attending to him. She pleaded with me to leave so that he could rest a little bit more, but Parsons persuaded her to allow me stay a while longer.

Pointing to the manuscript, I told him I was almost through but needed to ask him a few questions for clarity. Regarding the story of his visit to the Badagry slave post, however, I asked if there was any possibility that Granma Senami might still be alive to tell this story on camera. The way I felt, I would have given anything to be able to have her account on record, including the old slave town, holding areas, shackles, everything.

"Let's see, Carl" Parsons said, pondering (or so I thought) over the possibility of helping to make this happen. "In the early 70s when I had the encounter with Granma Senami, she was believed to be well over a hundred years old at the time. No one knew her exact age, and I can bet she didn't either. However, if we really put our mind to it, I think we might probably run into her at one of the local fitness centers in Badagry working as the world's oldest and only toothless aerobics instructor."

We talked for some time, and I realized he was struggling to stay awake – eyelids shutting intermittently and obviously becoming increasingly slow in reopening. My mind went back to the way he looked when I saw him in that old building just outside of town tied to a chair. Maybe it was because Tanya had drawn my attention to it, but it was obvious he was in dire distress. He was sweating a lot, and apparently had difficulty breathing. His hands and legs were abnormally swollen, and they left a depression that lasted a while if one applied a little pressure with the fingers. This was later described by the nurses as a pitting edema. It was a good thing we got him some medical attention when we did.

I left him to sleep and went back to a nice quiet spot in the hospital waiting room to finish reading Parsons' manuscript. The rest of it was a very vivid account of his ordeal in the hands of my buddies – the combination of Kareem, Athiel, Tanya, Ali and Mo. This was the first time I got an insight into what my buddies had put him through, and I could only shake my head in pity trying to imagine how he must have felt. Below is a part of what Parsons wrote about his experience:

...However hard I tried, it seemed I just couldn't get my eyes to stay open. There was this gentle breeze blowing steadily from "Lord knows where" that seemed to get steadily colder. And, except for a dim light that was flickering somewhere in the distance, my immediate environment was almost totally dark.

As I slipped in and out of consciousness, I recalled that it was about a week to another long Labor Day weekend. After much ado, Irene and her husband had finally convinced me that we should all go and spend the upcoming Labor Day holiday at their ranch. A few summers ago, I had spent a couple of weeks doing some work on that beautiful piece of real estate. Another invitation from Irene to visit the ranch again was just too tempting to decline. In comparison to the big city, the environment and scenery at the ranch was like paradise – simply breath-taking from almost every part of the house. Since then, I had been longing to go back, even if it was only for a few days. Anyway, without any persuasion whatsoever, you could say that I finally gave in.

Later on that day, I grabbed my sports bag and headed for the YMCA to meet the guys for our regular game of racquetball. A group of five of us played racquetball regularly, about three times a week, on set days. I won a game and lost two, to too many unforced errors.

I remembered leaving the YMCA Club after another exhausting evening feeling really good. One after the other, each one of us left the club after checking with the other guys to ensure that we would meet on Sunday afternoon after church.

It was about 8.30 pm, and just as I was looking into the side pocket of my sports bag for my car keys, this beautiful black lady had come up to me smiling. She introduced herself as Karen and, very politely, asked if I could help figure out what was wrong with her car. Even after numerous attempts, she said, her car would not start (pointing to a car parked about fifty yards away). I was no auto mechanic or expert, but the little I knew gave me enough confidence to see if there was any quick or temporary fix to her car problem.

"Sure," I replied, remembering that I had seen the lady a couple of times recently on the premises of the YMCA. A fine lady in distress, I thought. I didn't require much persuasion to go and see what I could do to help, and probably get to know her better.

She walked me towards a fairly new AMC Pacer and handed me a small bunch of keys that included the key to the car. I remembered opening the driver's door to get into the driver's seat, inserted the key into the ignition, and then all hell broke loose. I felt a powerful arm come across and pin my neck to the headrest, at the same time I felt the coldness of steel at my temple. The man asked me to relax so that the situation would not get any messier. In the meantime, the lady had pulled out a little syringe and injected its content into the side of my neck even as I was pleading with her not to. That was the last thing I remembered from that encounter at the Club.

I found myself struggling to put the pieces together in my head, trying to figure out the motive behind the incident in the parking lot. Who was that terrible woman and who was, or were, her accomplices? Gosh. Some of the most dangerous things come in the most beautiful packages.

Still feeling somewhat weak and groggy as I became more conscious, I patted the space around me, with the faintest of hopes that I would feel that lovely duvet that never failed to provide the warmth I craved for on cold nights. Instead of grabbing a soft duvet, my hands were filled with a loose and grainy substance which turned out to be ... loose soil. I raised my head slightly to look at each of my hands to actually confirm what I already knew was some kind of soil.

If it was a dream, at that point in time I was really ready to wake up. However, something (most probably the drug that had been injected into my body) kept me from becoming fully alert. I just couldn't get up without a great deal of effort, and I was so cold. I let go of the soil in my hands and ran my hands over my torso and arms. They were bare – no vest, and no shirt. Whoever those people were that took me, also took my vest and shirt. It was definitely not my style to sleep without any clothes on. One thing was becoming very clear and very quickly too. This was not a dream at all.

The powerful combination of anxiety, curiosity and the growing discomfort was compelling enough to keep me from slipping into slumber again. Hazy as my mind still was, I managed to open my eyes and stay awake long enough to begin the task of finding out more about my environment, and just how much of a predicament I was in. I had no clue where I was because nothing around me was familiar. Where was I really, or where could I possibly be right now in this vast country? Considering I had no idea how long I had been unconscious, the possibility existed that I could have been transported anywhere by my assailants.

Still somewhat bewildered, I raised my torso with the support of my elbows, while I looked down at the rest of my body. I had nothing on except my underpants and my pair of socks. Awake or still fast asleep, things were not looking good at all. A nightmarish scenario was beginning to unfold. If someone was playing a very bad practical joke on me, I certainly wasn't finding it funny.

In an attempt to sit up and draw my knees towards my chest, the action came to an abrupt halt about halfway through the motion accompanied by a sharp pain at my ankles. Instinctively, I felt compelled to move my butt forward to find out what had caused the pain and also restrained me at the ankles. There were metal-like clamps around my ankles secured by what I recognized to be padlocks. But, hold on a second right there, I thought. Why would anyone put clamps around my ankles?

I was almost certain that I was mistaken. It was still a little dark, but my eyes were steadily getting accustomed to my surroundings. The two ankle clamps were secured to a chain, which I traced over a distance of about fifteen feet to a wall. "Dear Lord," I must have said aloud. Something was definitely wrong with that picture. I was trying to figure out if the content of the syringe had actually killed me, or maybe I was having the worst nightmare ever.

Somehow, even though my mind still remained clouded, drifting between the state of wakefulness and sleep, I felt reasonably hopeful that everything was going to be alright. I did feel assured that I wasn't dead, though; at least not yet.

But for the chains around my ankles, it would have been easy to imagine that I had been pronounced dead, gotten buried and had just woken up inside my grave. That really would have been most unfortunate indeed.

After noticing that there was a flight of stairs that led up to a door, I quickly figured that I was confined in a cellar with an unfinished floor. Through the slats in the floor above, I could see a dim light flickering somewhere in the room above from where there seemed to be a lot of activity.

All of a sudden, the door at the top of the stairs opened and down came four men and a lady. It was the same lady who had pretended she had car trouble at the YMCA. All the men wore Mardi Gras-type masks obviously to conceal their identity, while one of them carried what looked like a doctor's bag. They were all Black guys, but none of them said a word to me. Upon a hand signal, three of the men came over to restrain me while the guy with the doctor's bag was assisted by the lady in filling up a syringe from some vials of medicine. Not again, I thought. I tried to resist as hard as I could to no avail, while still demanding information about the content of the syringe.

Nothing to worry about, he answered, assuring me that he was a certified physician as if that gave him the right to inject me with a drug I neither needed nor requested. According to him, the shot was necessary because we were going on a voyage back through time so that he could teach me a few important lessons. I couldn't make sense of what he was saying, but he went ahead and gave me a jab anyway, right in my neck – again.

Regarding the entire incident, the first thought that had come to my mind was that I had been abducted for ransom. Judging by the level of education of my abductors, it became obvious that I was in the hands of some radicals who had an axe to grind with me. In a way, that thought seemed to ring true, but I was becoming overwhelmed with sleep to make any sense of the fragments of events and pictures that were floating around in my head.

As I struggled for clarity within my mind, I wondered who these masked men were. For two reasons, I felt a little assured that they had no intention to kill me. If they did, I thought, there would have been no need for them to conceal their identities, and no one can teach a dead man any lessons. By this time, there was no doubt in my mind that this whole thing was connected to opinions I had expressed publicly about slavery and the slave trade. What lessons were they hoping to teach me, and how? I guessed I was going to find out sooner than later.

My head was throbbing and my heart was pounding heavily as the self-proclaimed doctor's voice filled my head with all sorts of things. He started to talk about family – a wife and kids – and a home, and a lot of other things that were completely strange to me. He told me that I needed to wake up from my dream to embrace the reality of the trauma I had gone through with my family and so many others. Through the conflicting thoughts running through my mind, I began to see pictures of a family in the setting of a tropical paradise.

It was about mid-morning, and I had just returned from clearing the weed from the crops in my farm. I could see my kinsmen going about their duties, while the women were on the way to the market to buy what would be required to prepare food for their different households. The palm-wine tappers were just climbing down from the tall palm trees, from which they were bringing down strategically-placed kegs into which the sweet, yeast-rich sap had seeped slowly from the break of dawn. Very soon, deliveries of fresh palm-wine would be made straight from Mother Nature to the homes of all the big shots in the village. Yes, this was home alright, and everything was the way it was supposed to be.

How could I have imagined that I was not married and that I had no children? Of course, I do. I remembered them going in and out of the house performing their daily chores. I always went to the farm early in the morning with my son to plant, clear the weeds, and perform any other necessary tasks. Then he would go back home to feed the goats and chickens at the back of the hut. I could see my daughter on her way back from the well as usual, where she would go to fetch water for the big clay pots at home.

All of a sudden, powerful memories about my family and kinsmen kept flooding my befuddled mind. What could possibly have happened to make me forget my entire life? As if looking through a family album, the pictures and thoughts became really vivid. I sank in dejection onto the bare earth beneath me, and covered my face with my hands in shame. Pray for them, something said within me, and I began to pray. As sleep finally appeared to be winning over wakefulness, it occurred to me that I had sub-consciously blocked out memories of family and kinfolk on account of the serious trauma we had all suffered.

[Even at that point, I must tell you, there were a couple of times when I was so sure that these scenarios were a part of a terrible nightmare from which I could not wake up. The tour of the Badagry relics of the slave trade, coupled with all the different stories I had read over the years about slavery and the slave trade, had been a sobering experience that I found hard to erase from my memories for a very long time. So, it was hard to tell if the combination of these things had left a very deep impression on my mind. It also occurred to me that another explanation could be that I was reliving the experiences of a past life, as reincarnation advocates might suggest. But then, everything seemed so real I had to let go of any thoughts that suggested otherwise.]

I found myself completely consumed as the 'recollection' of certain scenarios and events completely dominated my mind. Yes, it all seemed to come back to me – a lovely wife called Korede, a lovely fourteen year old daughter Titilope, and a sixteen year old son, Tomiwa. Where were they, really? Would I ever see them again, I kept asking myself. The word "never" kept popping up in my mind.

I remember attacking the shackles on my ankles furiously as I became overwhelmed by panic. The more futile my efforts proved, the more the tears that filled up my eyes and rolled down my cheeks. I should be thankful, an inner voice told me. The chains, as I thought I recalled, had been on my neck – almost choking me to death each time some-one fell or made a wrong turn. This suggested that I had not been alone. So, where are the others, and why couldn't I remember? All sorts of questions and thoughts were racing feverishly through my mind, and there was no-one around to provide any answers.

Probably the only thing that prevented the "lid" from being blown off the top of my head from severe anxiety was this soothing inner voice that kept urging me to calm down, with the assurance that everything would turn out just fine. Probably the worst part of the entire situation was that the lines between reality, imagination and a dream had not just been blurred, they had been totally erased. It seemed as if I was asleep when I was awake, and that I was awake when I thought I was fast asleep. And, sometimes, it felt like I was awake and asleep at the same time.

As I saw it, my area of confinement allowed only a crouching movement for anyone taller than about five feet six inches, or maybe five feet nine inches. A few yards away, there was a metal grille behind which were two rusty and battered tin cups. They contained what appeared to be rain water that had filled the cups over a period of time. My throat was so parched, I felt the urge to grab the cups and start drinking. Somehow, the urge to drink yielded to the great curiosity to understand the nature and extent of my predicament. Beside the cups was a banged-up aluminum plate containing ... left-over food? In the plate was a stale loaf of bread slightly larger than a grown adult fist with some red beans.

In a rather funny way, I found myself craving for that stale loaf of bread and beans with the same gusto you would expect of someone who was near death from starvation. I couldn't understand why it felt as if I had not eaten in days. It didn't look good at all, but I was ready to devour it with relish — even with some mold already growing on it. Something within me said that was the least of my problems at that moment. It was food, and that was all that mattered. Even with what I thought were little dead insects, or not, inside the red beans, that was what was available for the moment.

In an effort to quench my thirst, I remember trying to decide which cup to drink from. One or two little creatures darted across the surface of the water in the tin cups, while some dived (like submarines) towards the bottom of both cups. Upon a slight hesitation, the 'voice of reason' suggested that this was not the time to pay any attention to such 'minor' details. After all, this was not unlike trying to drink water from a village stream that was shared by small to large creatures. Many times, you needed to wave your hand over the area you from which you wanted to drink in order to allow the smaller creatures to either dive or fly away. All you had to do was time the interval between the creatures' dives, and then take a fast sip of the water. You just had to be patient to repeat the process if you were very thirsty. However, the biggest mistake you could make was to linger on every sip.

I had no idea how long had I been in that ... dungeon? Though I had never seen, or been in, a dungeon before, the word kept coming to my mind as a fitting description for where I had found myself. "Hello, hello" I must have shouted a number of times, but there was no response. Except for the clanking of my chains, there was just dead silence, if such a thing exists in the universe.

Without any warning whatsoever, I felt a sharp pain in my head and I could almost hear my heart beating faster than usual. Every other thought in my mind vanished, to be replaced by a clear recollection of my family, kinsmen, and the terrible events that apparently changed our lives forever.

The drama that led to where I found myself started to unfold and it was, as they say, out of this world. Words fail me in describing our ordeal at the hands of a swarm of mysterious and strange-looking characters. And there I was, half-nude, bathing in the tropical sun and minding my own business, when all hell broke loose. No one could tell whether or not they were wearing masks, but their skin-color was different and their clothing was very strange. Both children and adults alike were petrified from gazing upon their features – cold eyes of different colors, huge noses, and hair that resembled a horse's or lion's mane.

Nobody was safe from these marauders – they were vicious and cruel to men, women and children alike. Nobody knew what was going on. They hunted everyone down the way we hunted small and large animals for food and other uses. Those they caught were bound like pigs being prepared for slaughter.

With strong but strange bracelets around our hands and necks, these strange men herded us like goats and cows from our homes all the way down to the waterside. There we were — Chieftains, strong leaders of major households and proud husbands — helplessly trying to avoid the looks of horror and disbelief on our wives' and daughters' faces as the strangers forcefully had sex with them.

These beasts had no patience or sympathy with the virgins who screamed endlessly, only to be left in severe pain and in pools of blood that was proof of their virginity and purity. One of those virgins was my own teenage daughter, Titilope. She screamed my name over and over, begging to be rescued from the "masquerade from the world of the dead", and I just died over and over and over again because I was powerless to help her.

Even though she was restrained not far from me, both of us avoided each other's gaze out of shame. For my daughter, a taboo had been broken by what I had to witness. For me, it was shameful that I had failed in my duty as a father to protect my own child. That was the kind of day that a proud father never prays to be alive to witness. It would have been better for people to say that "such an incident would never have occurred if her father was alive".

Sadder still, I was too well restrained to make any attempts to take my own life. I begged everyone — captors and other captives — to please take my life or give me a knife to slice my own throat. No one heeded my call. The colored devils chattered aloud in their strange language and laughed at the different ways we expressed our sorrow, pain and discomfort. We had no clue what lay ahead of us, like sheep been led to the slaughter.

For days we were kept in pits without food, while more and more people were brought from different villages, towns and tribes — many completely naked in front of their children and former neighbors — and pushed into the pits that were already overcrowded. From there we were loaded, like merchandise, into very big boats that sailed farther and farther away from the shores of our motherland to the place where the heavens meet the mighty waters. Slowly, what was left of our motherland receded from sight as Yemoja, the Queen of the mighty ocean, constantly protected the big boat from being swallowed into her bosom.

Who were these people? No one among them spoke a language that we could understand or remember ever hearing before.

For long moments at a time, there was just silence among us. Even the great Juju men and women had become impotent, and were also at the mercy of the foreigners. Hope was fading faster than any spells that were being cast by the Juju priests. Fathers had also been rendered impotent as they were held captive along with their children and the mothers of their children. Our young daughters and wives were repeatedly sexually assaulted, sometimes right there in front of everybody.

The first time one of the captors 'took' my wife – in full view of all other captives – she kept asking if I was going to do nothing but watch another man rob her of respect and dignity, particularly under the full gaze of her son, daughter, neighbors and total strangers. What, really, could I do? That was my wife, my life and my love – the mother of my children, and a member of a royal family – ravaged like a common whore without any dignity. When that bastard finished with her, she remained on the floor – quiet and with thighs still wide open. Most of the other captives, against the advice of some of the elders, nearly killed themselves trying to get an uninterrupted look at my wife's genitalia. Even worse, rather than being horrified, most of the sorry bastards from other tribes and villages were clearly aroused – even under our seriously pitiful conditions.

What could I have done, except to pray for the ground to open up and swallow me into its' belly to be seen no more by man or God. Since the same thing had happened to the wives, daughters and sisters of other men, I was sure that this dreaded day would come. I had no doubt my wife felt the same way also. I am also certain that we both prayed independently that the gods would intervene to prevent it from happening.

Anyway, I had to summon the strength and courage to call out to her. I pleaded with her to please get up and cover herself, while invoking the gods to let dogs feed on our captors while they were still alive to feel the pain and the shame.

After a few minutes, still without saying a word but with tears streaming down her eyes, she finally got up. She moved away to a darker part of the belly of the huge boat. I could hear her sobbing, notwithstanding the chatter among fellow captives and the noise of the ocean as it lashed viciously and relentlessly at the oversized boat. Such events became commonplace, but nothing was more shocking than the fact that some of the young boys were not spared the abomination of sexual assaults.

As time passed, those who became too sick from injuries sustained during capture, or from other diseases, were almost destined for a watery grave. The unfortunate ones who died or were too sick to go on were thrown into the great waters in the middle of nowhere. We had to plead with those who were getting ready to pass out that it was not in their best interest to do so. We propped them up to the best of our collective dwindling ability. Led by some brave women, we resolved to sing spiritually uplifting songs as opposed to singing dirges for the dead.

But, where were the gods to strike down these colored devils and set us free to roam our dear native lands? Were we ever going to see our homes and families again?

Most of the women and some of the young men cried and asked us (their fathers and other elders) for answers which we could not provide. Some fell very sick from the movement of the big oceans, and there was nothing we could do to help them. You could see the respect for former Chieftains and elders slowly diminish in the eyes of those who previously held them in very high esteem. Powerful men, who strode like lions through the villages and towns and evoked trembling from young and old alike, were now trapped and encaged like little rodents. What was going on? We couldn't tell then and still can't tell now; and the answers will probably elude us for the rest of our lives. Of course, that was assuming any one of us survived to tell the story.

There was very little food and water to go around. And, when it was provided, it was a show of shame to see former men of honor in a scramble with boys and girls who used to look up to them – all in a desperate bid for less than a mouthful of food or water. Despite the scarcity, however, there were a few men and women who still gave up their food and water for the benefit of the sick and the young, sometimes going for days with barely anything to eat.

There was no space or time to get sufficient sleep. There was a great deal of apprehension any time strange sounds were heard, when huge doors were slammed shut, and particularly when the weather turned very harsh. The air was so cold you could hear all our teeth chattering from a mile away, considering many of us were either scantily clad or completely naked.

The air was filled with wails and moans and endless prayers to the gods for mercy – mercy that some received only in the form of death. The permanent grip and smell of death filled the air just as much as the stench of defecation did. Both smells refused to go away, and both lingered with us for the entire journey.

Brothers died in front of their sisters, husbands died in front of their wives and children, wives and daughters were taken out sometimes never to be seen again. That was the daily pattern. I saw those who were merely boys become men in the face of extreme adversity, and I witnessed women rising up to play the role of those who were previously defined and described as men.

All the men and women who were taken out at odd hours of the night to do one thing or another came back with strange stories of the devilish practices and powers of the colored strangers. Some of them also came back with food, as reward for various services, for their loved ones. No one knew the extent of the range of services they rendered, but the news was that they were mostly sexual in nature.

After what seemed to be an eternity, we finally saw land again. We felt both joy and sadness – joy for finally setting foot on solid ground again, and sadness because this land was filled with many more of the colored devils. There were also many other big and small boats. Everybody looked alike, and you could hardly tell one from the other. Those strange people looked at us with as much curiosity as we had looking at them. It was clear that some were also as afraid of us as some of us were afraid of them. Going by how cold the air was, it was easy to understand why they were all covered up very strangely.

The shame, for want of a better word, was profound to say the least. There we were – chieftains and warriors who had gained a reputation of being as solid as the immovable Iroko and Obeche trees back home – mostly completely naked in a strange land and with remarkable (and not so remarkable) "pendulums" on public display.

People pinched their noses shut because we stunk worse than he-goats, and made haste to create a safe distance from us as we were herded like wild animals past them. We knew we stunk to high heavens and, even if you were free, you could not run away from yourself.

The beautiful ebony skins of most of my people were caked-over as if with dirt from over a hundred years. Water had been scarce to come by even for drinking, let alone bathing. Taking a shower had become a luxury that was accorded to the women and boys with whom our captors fulfilled their sexual desires, and to anyone who was assigned certain special duties on the boat.

Since we had no access to 'chewing sticks' with which we brushed our teeth, some of us seized every opportunity to rinse our mouths with the seawater that frequently lashed at the boat. It was not good enough, but our captors had not given us the courtesy or privilege of preparing for the unwanted and forced boat trip. Many of us had developed various skin diseases and illnesses that were both familiar and totally unknown to us. Infections and fevers were rampant. Old sores and wounds festered with pus because they went untreated.

Cleaning up after a bowel movement was a big problem. Back home, this was achieved by using water, or leaves where water was not available. On the boat, there was no water and there were no leaves. And, maybe because our captors did not care to carry enough supplies, or because there were not enough buckets to handle the frequency and volume of waste from bowel movements in the over-crowded boat, we were sustained just below starvation. After all, if there wasn't enough food in your system, there would be little or nothing for your bowels to move.

Anyway, on arrival in that strange land, you could not convince most of the men and women that we were all actually not dead and just didn't know it. After all, how else could one explain all that had happened? If indeed we were dead, some asked, were we in heaven or deep in the bosom of hell? The response of the Chieftains to that question was almost unanimous – "very soon, we shall know".

We were all divided into different groups and herded like goats into strange dwellings with doors that led into the earth like graves. The foreigners were talking in their strange language and walking on top of us as if we were dead and buried. Maybe we were, or may we should have been. But, that was the last day I laid eyes on my wife and children, or ever heard from them.

It was at this place that we were kept for long periods of time until we were taken to the surface for examination and traded in the same manner that we traded livestock in the markets back home. So, in ones, twos, or more, our numbers were depleted as men and women were bound and taken away by different people into uncertainty.

Nightfall brought little or no sleep, regardless of the form of labor to which we were put from sun-up till sun-down. How could anyone have slept well on near-empty stomachs, or when they had no idea what was going to happen to them the following day?

It must have been my imagination, but there were days and nights I thought I heard a voice that sounded so much like my wife's in the near distance. The voice was loud enough for me to hear her pleas against repeated sexual assaults, followed by periods of uncontrollable sobbing. On many occasions, and at different times, something within me suggested that I call out to the gentle voice to offer some consolation. The real intention was to confirm whether or not the voice was actually Korede's. To my dismay, however, there was never any answer; the sobbing would just slowly fade away and all would be still once more. Did I hear the distressed voice of my wife calling out my name? I could have sworn I did.

After a while, to preserve my sanity, I had to stop calling out to the voice and try to occupy my head with silly things, or attempt to block my ears with my fingers. At some point later, the sobbing stopped; and so did the sounds of resistance, even though I thought I could still hear voices faintly in the distance, as if in short conversation. Maybe my wife, or to whomever the voice belonged, had finally taken the path of least resistance. She had been given no choice but to resign herself to fate in the hands of her captors.

But, was it actually Korede or not? If it was not my wife, it was definitely another woman; one that seemed to be there against her will. Then, an inner voice rebuked me for daring to refer to her as my wife. Did I not lose that right or privilege when I failed to protect her from wanton sexual assaults and humiliation, I asked myself. I could hear the voice of the gods telling me that I had lost the right to call myself a man, the father of any children, or any woman's husband.

The options were not many, said the voice within me, and none was going to be easy. I could pray to the gods to grant me the courage to take my own life, so that I could come back in another life to avenge all these wrongs. On the other hand, I could pray that the gods would be merciful enough to take my life and bring me back in another life as the 'woman' into which these foreign devils had already turned me.

Indescribable but intense rages swelled up within my body so many times and so quickly that I thought I was going to burst major blood vessels or just simply explode.

Going through my mind were crazy thoughts, as if the gods did not want me to miss the import of every single event. How can any wife ever have respect for a husband who stands helpless and watches as she is ravaged by another man? Even when she stops screaming your name for help and the tears stop flowing on the outside, you know without a doubt that she would still be crying inside. She would know that you can hear her, and that you can feel her disappointment. From that moment on, you become no more than a boy to your own wife – one who no longer has any pride or integrity to claim the authority of being the head of any household.

What could be more effective in destroying the core and pride of family? Did I miss the fact that our captors had succeeded in eroding the respect that wives had for their husbands and the respect that the children had for their parents? No. Or, did I not notice how those of us who were fathers, mothers, daughters and sons avoided eye-contact with, or completely avoided, one another out of shame? Men who were once heroes with auras of invincibility had been reduced to grasshoppers. These foreigners had turned all our lives completely inside out...

The foregoing account, according to Parsons, were the images or impressions created in his mind by Athiel, aided by Kareem and others. In reality, Parsons had never been married and he had no children. I had no doubt that Athiel was the mastermind behind Parsons' kidnapping and mental torture. Everything pointed to Athiel. Kareem and Tanya did not have the depth and capacity to plan and execute a scheme as complex as this. It was the kind of stuff that you read in novels about secret agents and government organizations. Maybe there was a lot more to Athiel Brownidge than many of us cared to imagine.

As I said earlier on, Athiel Brownidge was said to have worked on the medical team of a Non-Profit Organization — whose name he never disclosed — that provided medical services and supplies to places in Central and Southern Africa and the Far East. On one of those few occasions when he talked, he had revealed his fascination with mind-control and hypnotism — drug-induced and otherwise. He said that he had witnessed demonstrations and various applications of mind-control that left him speechless.

The only examples he gave us were about witnessing a local medicine-man either blow-darting people, or touching certain parts of their body with locally crafted implements to produce very strange reactions in them. The effects, he said, ranged from making them feel like they were freezing in the heat of the tropics, making others behave and believe that they possessed superhuman strength, or just helping warriors overcome pain and believing in their invincibility. Talking about these unorthodox but apparently effective techniques and secrets of 'mind-control' got him unusually animated.

He concluded by saying that the human mind is a powerful and incredibly fathomless thing. "You could live an entire life and die within it without having to leave the same spot. It holds the secrets to the human capability to have dominion over all things as scriptural writings say. Depending on the capacity of one's mind, it is easy for a man to become a giant among his fellowmen or, regardless of his size, be a little man among those much smaller in size than he is. I have absolutely no doubt that a great and mighty power lurks within each of our fathomless minds."

CHAPTER FIVE

THE KANGAROO COURT

Parsons account of his ordeal was shocking, to say the least. What was even more shocking was the fact that members of our organization – professionals in every regard – were involved in something so outrageous and criminal. Worse still, I had been given no clue as to what was going on. Of course, the whole thing came to an end, and in good time too, the very first day I was brought into the picture. That Wednesday morning could not have shown or prepared me for what the rest of that day would throw at me.

The telephone extension in the office I shared with three others lit up, and the receptionist announced that I had a guest waiting in the lobby. Who could my early morning visitor be? It couldn't be my wife, So-so, because the receptionist would have allowed her to proceed directly to my office. I remember checking my watch – it wasn't even ten o'clock yet – and I was already so engrossed in preparing a response to a lawsuit on behalf of one of the firm's clients. I remember being curious to see who it was and, at the same time, reluctant to leave what I was doing.

In the waiting room was one of Tanya Hume's friends, Tilly. She handed me a sealed envelope addressed by Tanya and marked urgent, then turned around to leave. I was a little worried because Tanya had never had cause to write to me before. I asked Tilly if Tanya was okay, and if she had any clue about the subject matter. She smiled, assured me that Tanya was okay, and continued towards the door.

The note in the envelope started with a strong plea from Tanya that I should not disclose to anyone how I got the information she was passing on to me. According to her, something very serious was going on that involved her fiancé, Athiel Brownidge, Kareem Hamada, Mo Harvey and Ali Johnson. I soon discovered that she was also deeply involved with the same guys in the rather 'sinister' activity that was about to be revealed to me.

In her note, Tanya was worried that "the guy is very sick and I am afraid he might die if we don't do something soon". She also included an address located in an older part of the city that was being bought up by new investors for redevelopment, and suggested that I should try to be there by about six o'clock that evening.

If that envelope had been delivered by someone else besides Tilly, I would have drawn the conclusion that this was a sick joke. From documents I had seen within our organization, I recognized the handwriting to be Tanya's, but the note made no sense whatsoever. Who was the sick guy that was likely to get killed, why and by whom? And who constituted "we" that could possibly do anything to prevent some sick guy from being killed by whom? Why didn't Tanya or any of the guys go to the police?

Hakeem recently acquired an old three bedroom property in the same neighborhood for one of his many business associates. He had been working on hooking up his business partners with realtors for lucrative real estate deals in the area. When we both went to view the property, he had said that the proposed buyer was either going to try and salvage it, or have it pulled down completely if it was found to be structurally unsound. At that moment, I just couldn't figure out if the address in Tanya's note was the same property I had viewed with Hakeem, or another property.

The problem I needed to solve was how to go about "stumbling" on something that I was not supposed to know about in the first place. I felt a little disappointed that Kareem, as close as I thought we were, would be involved with Athiel, Mo, Ali and Tanya in 'something' so confidential for it not to be mentioned to me. With Mo and Ali, I really never cared to know what mischief they were up to. However, with Athiel and Tanya in the loop on whatever they had going on at that time, there was no doubt in my mind that it would have to be something quite serious. Anyhow, I made a decision to handle the situation with a lot of caution and diplomacy. I made sure I left the office early enough and headed straight to the address in Tanya's note to be sure I was there for six o'clock.

I got to the location indicated in Tanya's note in my trusted 1975 Pontiac Astre at about 5.30 p.m., half an hour before the time suggested by her. The property was indeed the same one that I had viewed with Kareem. I drove past it to a spot, not too far away, where I could observe the goings-on at the property without being seen. Reclining the seat just a little, I turned off the engine and waited anxiously in my car. About ten minutes later, a familiar-looking rusty Chevrolet Vega Hatchback pulled up in front of the building. I saw Mo Harvey come out of the car with what looked like two small bags of groceries, walk up to knock on the front door, and it was opened to let him in. Who else was inside the old house? I could almost bet that Ali Johnson was inside that building and, if he wasn't, you could bet he would not be too far away. Mo and Ali were like the tortoise and its shell – you hardly ever saw one without the other.

At about ten minutes before six o'clock, Kareem appears in his two-tone 'super steed' (as he liked to call his 1969 Pontiac GTO Convertible) from around the corner with Athiel and Tanya in it. The three of them walked up to the front door, which Kareem unlocked to let them in. So, what next, I thought? Again, in my characteristic manner, I decided to approach the situation with a little caution and diplomacy.

I started the car, drove up to the building, walked up to the front door and simply knocked.

There was no answer, so I knocked a little harder. After all, I was certain that there were people in there – and those I had seen so far were my buddies. A couple of them act crazy sometimes because of the cannabis they could not stay away from smoking, but they were definitely not killers. But, who was the sick guy that was likely to die, and why? Something very serious was going on inside that derelict property, and I was now more determined than ever to find out what it was.

Kareem finally opened the door, came out quickly, and shut the door behind him just as quickly. Looking apparently flustered, he wanted to know what I was doing there. My response was brief: I was looking at property in the area for a client, thought I saw a car that looked like his, followed it, recognized the license plates, saw Athiel, Tanya and himself get out, and thought he was showing them the property just as he had showed it to me previously.

Kareem 'bought' the story, finally managed an unconvincing smile, and headed towards the street as if he was 'seeing me off'. I stayed right where I was at the entrance to the property, told him that I wasn't in a hurry, and that I would like to enter to say hello to our other friends. I could hear him muttering expletives under his breath as I made a move to go through the front door. He ran back and blocked me, and I looked at him questioningly. "What the heck is going on, Kareem? What is wrong with you?" I asked. He apologized, and tried to explain that there was some very serious business being conducted inside. When I told him that I was ready to wait till their serious business was concluded, he paced in circles for about twenty seconds, and pleaded with me to give him a couple of minutes.

Kareem dashed inside the old property, shut the door and I could hear the lock turn. He came back outside a few minutes later and said that I could come in on the condition that I would be calm, and stay out of sight in the kitchen area. He warned that I might find certain things disagreeable, but he promised to explain 'everything' later on. When I nodded to indicate that I 'got his drift', he allowed me to go in with him, and locked the door behind us.

Surprisingly, the property had been reasonably cleaned up and made somewhat habitable. The plates in the kitchen sink, the empty cans of beer and soda, groceries in the icebox and scraps of food, made it obvious that it was lived-in. Kareem then pulled me aside to suggest that I should be calm and wait out of sight in the kitchen. Calm, yes. Wait and remain out of sight in the kitchen, most definitely not. Being as close as we had been from our teenage years, Kareem should have known better than to suggest something like that. I walked slowly, and as softly as I could on those creaky old floor-boards, to the kitchen entrance to get a peek into the living area.

In the sparsely decorated living room were a love seat sleeper, a standing lamp, two wooden high stools, and a small dining table with three chairs. On the fourth dining-table chair, placed about five feet from the table, was a blindfolded mulatto male in boxer shorts and what obviously used to be a white t-shirt. I noticed that the man was barefooted. His hands were tied behind the back of the chair, his head was bowed, and he was sweating profusely. I had no clue what was going on yet, but that first peek didn't look good at all.

"Mr. Thomas Parsons," announced Athiel, in a setting that was more like some kangaroo court. "Your ability to adapt to a new environment was nothing short of remarkable. You surpassed all of our expectations. You can call me AB. I will be doing most of the talking, but I have a few others here who might wish to say something as we proceed." It was at that moment that I knew the identity of the blindfolded mulatto tied up to the chair. Mo Harvey and Ali Johnson, certified morons as far as I was concerned, were unashamedly perched on two high stools behind that poor guy like they were guards.

"As you might have gathered already, we have absolutely no intention of taking your life. Our only purpose is to help make you a little more sensitive to the plight of the Black community from the time the White man took our ancestors out of their God-given land in Africa against their will. I do not think it would be incorrect for members of the Black community to say that the criminal actions and uneducated utterances of White supremacists and bigots continue to destroy our humanity, and the goals and aspirations of young Black men and women."

Thomas Parsons remained silent and, with chin dropped to his chest, shook his head almost unnoticeably. As the scenario unfolded, still to my utter disbelief, I had to struggle very hard to calm down to see if there was more to come. Was I dreaming or was it really true that a man had been kidnapped and probably tortured on account of perceived offensive racial comments?

"Do you agree with that assessment or do you not, Mr. Parsons?" Parsons raised his head and asked, with an incredulous smile, "Is this really what this is all about? Everybody knows about the Ku Klux Klan. I guess this must be the Black version of the KKK – the Cuckoo Klan. Isn't that just great?"

Athiel ignored Parsons' comments and continued, "Over time, people like you have engaged in propaganda against Blacks. White people, whose butts people like you love to kiss, continue to rob and deny Black men, women and children of the respect and opportunities that will replace fear and uncertainty with the faith and confidence they need to face a continuously challenging world."

Parsons and I must have been the only ones in that room who were wondering if the whole thing was a bad dream from which we would all wake up very, very soon.

Athiel tried again, "We hear you are authoring a book titled "Not Guilty", scheduled for release in the very near future, right?"

"That's correct," was Parsons' response, readjusting his posture on the chair and looking towards the sound of Athiel's voice as if he could actually see him.

"In almost every public event where you tried to promote your upcoming book, Mr. Parsons, you belittled the contributions of Dr. Reverend Martin Luther King Jr. to the black community, and you expressed opposition to affirmative action as a necessary tool for Blacks to achieve some degree of fairness and true equality in this society. Also, you showed no sensitivity whatsoever for the memory and suffering of our ancestors who were taken out of Africa in bondage and subjected to the most horrific treatment at the hands of their White captors and slave owners."

"What you went through these several days," he went on, "was designed to enable you experience and appreciate the dehumanization suffered by our ancestors at the hands of their captors. Those captors, of course, represent a part of your ancestry – the part that you favor over and above your 'lowly' Black ancestors. However, it is not our intention to resort to the sort of barbaric acts that have come to be identified with your White relatives. I wish we could apologize for interrupting your life in this manner, but that apology would bear no sincerity. What you were made to experience here was intended to teach you a valuable lesson; one which will forever be etched in your memory. For as long as you live, those memories are now yours. You now own them in the same way that our ancestors did. It is my hope that you will live with those horrible memories for a very long time."

I could not believe that I was standing in the same space with people who were in the middle of an ongoing criminal act. These crazy guys had actually kidnapped a man who had merely been exercising his constitutional freedom to express an opinion. The whole thing was wrong – very wrong. There had never been any doubt in my mind that the treatment of Blacks in the hands of Whites was wrong, but two wrongs will not make things right.

Parsons asked if he would eventually be allowed to respond.

"You'll have plenty of time to respond when I am done, Mr. Parsons. As I was saying, our ancestors were hounded like animals and forcefully taken from their natural environment to foreign lands to serve the needs of White people. Even before they left the shores of their motherland, the torture and dehumanization had already weakened them and compromised their health. Without any aid given or mercy shown, many succumbed during the hazardous journeys. Along with those who were still alive but seriously weakened from unending cruelty and torture at the hands of their White captors, they were thrown overboard and sent to watery graves. For those who survived to reach the shores of your foreign countries, the cruelty, torture and dehumanization continued unabated.

"From the moment you were brought here, Mr. Parsons, you were under very close observation. At first you didn't know where you were, and you found yourself caged like a captured animal in a hole dug out from the soil, just as your ancestors did to ours. With chains and shackles around your ankles, you experienced the kind of disorientation, dehumanization and humiliation that our ancestors did."

Athiel continued, "Do you remember how many times you cried out to God or someone to reach out to you like a human being, and got no response? You felt like a caged animal that so badly wanted to know if it was going to live or die. That was how our ancestors must have felt. You cried for mercy at every opportunity throughout this experiment for so many reasons, particularly when it became obvious that you had no control over the well-being or otherwise of your family. Like an animal, you were ready to drink bad water, eat bad food and live with the stench and filth of your own defecation."

Tanya got up from the dining table and walked towards the kitchen. She grabbed a soda and leaned close to whisper in my ear. "Look at his feet – they are badly swollen. They were not like that when he first got here. He sweats a lot and has difficulty breathing. Athiel says he suspects Parsons has some sort of a heart disease. I agree. He's been getting worse, but Athiel and Kareem are not taking it seriously enough."

Whose lame-brained idea was this anyway? How did it all start, and how long had Parsons been there? I had a million questions to ask. "Can't talk now," she replied, walking back, as if on egg-shells, to join Athiel and Kareem on the table. Even though I could see his legs from the knee down to his feet, I had never seen Thomas Parsons with his pants down. So, I really couldn't tell if there was any difference from what I was looking at, and what they used to be. However, if Athiel – a physician – admitted to his fiancé that there was a problem indeed, that was good enough for me.

Athiel continued to address an apparently unperturbed Parsons. He said that his White relatives considered our ancestors less than human and, till today, still treat their descendants as inferior to, or less human than, Caucasians. Athiel expressed the wish that many White people could be made to experience what Parsons did.

"I wish you could see how pathetic you looked," Athiel told Parsons. "Like an animal, you could not even clean yourself up after a bowel movement. It was interesting to watch you opt to save the little water you had for drinking, rather than use it for personal hygiene. And, throughout, you could not even stand erect like a human being. Anyone who attempts to downplay the suffering and humiliation of our ancestors should be thoroughly ashamed of themselves. In the same breath, anyone who underplays the fact that Black men and women are systematically beaten down physically and psychologically each time we try to get up is either plain ignorant or smoking something called 'stupid'."

"Wow", I thought. Even though I knew how passionate Athiel was about the plight of Blacks in this country, I had never seen this ... fanatical side of him. As I got to know later, Parsons had been held captive for about four days, and made to experience the suffering and human degradation of slavery (and the slave trade) through the eyes of a Black slave. In modified forms of slavery but no less evil, Athiel claimed, the descendants of Black slaves still have to fight discrimination, continuous degradation and the injustice of a White system that will not quit its wicked ways.

Athiel was on a roll as I had never seen him before. "We helped build most of these great modern Western cities. Their economies were developed with the sweat and blood of our ancestors. Our great ancestors also fought and died for peace and equality in this country – peace and equality that eluded them, and still elude their descendants till this day.

"Be rest assured that when 'class' is over, you will be reunited with your loved ones. That's the reason for the blindfold. It would not serve our purpose for any harm to come to you while you are our guest. Of course, that's a luxury your White relatives did not consider to extend to our ancestors. Did you know that about seventy five to eighty percent of White slave owners had female Black slaves as mistresses? In most cases, as if you didn't already know, they were unwilling mistresses. Our great grandmothers were raped at will literally in front of their husbands and children, and forced to indulge in the sexual fantasies and perversion of White men. Those women who were repeatedly violated were people's wives and mothers – our great, great-grandmothers. The men your White relatives humiliated and dehumanized were people's sons, husbands, and fathers – our great, great-grandfathers."

"You guys are sick, whoever you are. You need major help," Parsons' said, looking around the room even though he really couldn't see anyone through the blindfold. "Whoever you are, you guys are all messed up beyond your mothers' wildest nightmares. If you're not cowards, take off the blindfold and let us look straight into each other's eyes."

"That may be so, Mr. Parsons," Athiel responded, getting up to pace back and forth in front of Parsons as he continued to speak. In a tone that barely concealed his anger, Athiel stated slowly for emphasis, "We conceal our identities for your sake. It is the only way that we can feel comfortable to set you free once we are done with you. Should we feel reasonably concerned for the safety of any member of this team, we will not hesitate to take measures that we otherwise might not have intended. Fortunately for you, we are not as cold-blooded as the White men you've been sucking up to with your message. So far, any Black man with a message other than theirs has been assassinated."

To this day, I am almost certain that Parsons was able to see Athiel's feet from under the blindfold. There was no other way to explain what happened next, or the accuracy of the attack. As Athiel got within striking distance, Parsons' used an expletive, and his left leg went flying through the air towards Athiel's crotch. Wham. Or, crunch. Describe it how you will, but Parsons' made direct contact.

His foot connected very hard with Athiel's 'family jewels' in a way that could have sent his testicles coming out of his mouth, and he screamed out in excruciating pain. Each one of us in that room, even Tanya, must have felt that kick. I rushed out of my semi-concealment, just as Kareem got out of his chair, to help Athiel as he doubled over and fell to the floor grabbing his crotch with both hands. Tanya recovered from the shock and came running over to check on her fiancé's well-being (and most probably the viability of his 'assets').

In answer to our concerns, he tried to assure us that he was fine even though it was obvious he was still in a lot of pain. "It's okay, guys. I'm alright. I didn't figure him to be the violent type." We turned to look at Parsons only to discover that Ali Johnson had responded to the attack by going after Parsons. So, there he was, Parsons that is, knocked over to the side in his chair, blindfold lifted to expose his left eye, and staring intently at Ali Johnson. Kareem rushed over to pull down the blindfold over the exposed eye, but it could not be determined if Parsons had also caught a glimpse of him or not, or anybody else in the room.

"Many years ago, Parsons, your White ancestors would either have cut off the offending foot or merely taken your life to ensure there was no reoccurrence of such an act," Athiel said as he waddled back to his chair. "By the way, we are not cowards at all, Parsons. Our actions are unconventional and calculated to serve a specific purpose, but it is not designed to take your life. We are not killers. But, as I said earlier, that should not be interpreted to mean that there will be any hesitation on our part to take appropriate action, including having to take your life, should things get so terribly out of hand. That would be very unfortunate, Mr. Parsons."

Mo and Ali were trying to seat Parsons upright when he insisted on responding to Athiel's "rambling and the lopsidedness of the images and events he was made to experience." Without waiting for an answer, he said that the kick to Athiel's crotch was intended to inflict maximum damage to pay him back for injecting unknown substances into his body, and for the mental and physical ordeal to which he had been subjected. "Never in my wildest dreams did I imagine that my work or comments would elicit such feelings of extremism from supposedly educated minds.

"With all indignation, you have told me and fed my mind with your version of what White slave dealers and owners put your ancestors through. But, you missed the most crucial point regarding the profound involvement of their local African collaborators who had established reputations as slave dealers and headhunters. Willingly, the local strongmen facilitated slave trading to cater to the demands of the highest bidders, and it didn't matter who was buying – Arabs or Europeans. Hardly anyone says a word, or has tangible information, about the well-documented Trans Sahara slave trade by the Arabs. The Islamic nations of the Middle East bought or captured and sold many more Africans as slaves than all White nations combined.

"Nobody seems to know, or cares to be informed, that many more Africans were killed during the torturous journeys across the Sahara desert, the Red Sea and the Indian Ocean than on the hazardous transatlantic ocean voyages. The inhumane treatment suffered by African slaves at the hands of Western dealers and owners pales in comparison to what the Arab nations did to African slaves. Why is there so much anger, and finger-pointing, towards White folks than towards the Arabs who were even more mean to Blacks?

"The point to keep in mind at all times is that people – of any race or background – were simply ignorant, and they merely exhibited the savage-like tendencies and practices prevalent in human society in those times. Okay, consider this for a moment. Now that the Western world has made slavery and slave trading illegal, why does it still flourish in many parts of Africa, Asia, and the Middle East? Are White people responsible for the continuing capture, buying, and shipping of human beings for the purpose of enslavement?

"For heaven's sake, if you guys feel so loathsome of White folks and how this country treats you, why don't you catch any of the regularly available flights to the African homeland to see what you've been missing? I am so sick and tired of this racial nonsense.

"Listen. There is no doubt in my mind right now, and not that there ever was, that most Blacks have been through a lot in this country. But, does that give you justification, in these modern times, to kidnap people and torture them just to make a moot point? It grieves me greatly to see how the wonderful legacy of heroic Black men and women in world history is being squandered by the kind of misguided acts that many non-Blacks, justifiably or not, have labeled as being characteristic of Black people."

"Which misguided acts and what labels would that be?" asked Kareem in a tone that was laced with irritation at Parsons' comment.

"Can I be honest or would you just like me to blow smoke up your butts? I have a life-long policy, guys – nobody should ask me a serious question if they are not prepared for the answer." Parsons paused for a response, looking from one side of the room to the other, still blindfolded.

"Go on, Parsons, I don't imagine anyone of us would like to have smoke blown up our butts. Yeah. Honesty is good. First, tell us how Blacks are labeled by your White relatives," Kareem responded.

"Listen. There is a general opinion that most Blacks tend to be overly aggressive or violent, mostly lazy, and generally addicted to sponging off society. Those are not my words, but I have heard these terms used in White circles over and over again to describe most Black people." You could feel the chill in the room as the guys and Tanya adjusted themselves in their seats.

"Is that your opinion also?" Athiel asked, Parsons did not respond, and he continued. "Consider this. Would you not eventually get tired of being beaten into the ground each time you tried to get up? Would generation after generation not get tired of being pulled down again and again as would persons who keep slipping as they try to make it to the top of a sandy hill? Many of you are mistaken. Black people are not lazy, Mr. Parsons, they are just tired. Even though the line may be thin, there is still a world of difference between people who are generally lazy and those who eventually get tired of being constantly frustrated by a system originally designed to alienate them. The problem is that the system and the general attitudes of those who run the system are not changing quickly enough. As some have argued, these changes are not going to happen overnight. The same people who advance or support this argument should also realize that the genuine efforts of a lot of ambitious and hard-working

Blacks to stand on their own feet do get overwhelmingly frustrated by a system that appears bent on resisting change. If many of them give up and become rather laid-back, does that make them lazy and desirous only of sponging-off the nation? No, Mr. Parsons, I do not think so. It is my opinion that the purported "addiction" of Blacks to the pittance that 'welfare' offers is directly attributable to the crawl-mode of change of a system that was originally designed and made for Whites only. That being said, what are the misguided acts to which your White relatives refer?"

"Will my kidnapping qualify? Rather than make an effort to confront me with superior logic and facts, you have overreacted by expressing your disagreement with my opinion through violence and by committing a crime. Come on guys. Do I have to answer that question any more than that? Already, I am in a mess with you guys on account of opinions I expressed publicly. Why should I dig myself into a deeper hole? You do not seem like the kind of people with whom one can have a common-sense discussion. No, I am not going to answer that question any more than that," Parsons protested.

From the way we all exchanged looks, it was clear that Kareem, Athiel, Tanya and I were all pained by how Parsons' had characterized us. Athiel assured Parsons that we were prepared to entertain a discussion, and thus urged him to continue. And, continue Parsons did, regardless of the fact that he was still blindfolded, tied to a chair, and without a clue what his unknown captors would do next.

"With whom should you be more angry; the White men and Arabs who bought slaves or the ones who sold their own flesh and blood into slavery for self-enrichment? Do not be fooled by those soppy stories of how the White man came to raid towns and villages for slaves to cart away to Europe and elsewhere. Don't get me wrong, guys; I am not saying it did not happen in some cases. Even then, it was not without a significant amount of support and cooperation from local chieftains and slave dealers. The truth is that White slave traders had a full-blown business relationship with many traditional rulers and others whose prime occupation was to stalk and capture unguarded virile men and vulnerable women for sale.

"For your information, slavery still thrives in many parts of the world to this day; particularly in Africa. In most of these countries, slavery represents a very strong part of tradition and culture that date way back in history. In those days, the locals accepted it as a way of life that had existed for as long as anyone could tell, and many still see nothing wrong with that way of life even in present times. I know this not from rumors or newspaper articles, but from personal knowledge. But, we can get to the specifics later, if ever.

"Except there is any one of you who was born and raised in Africa, I believe I can say, with all confidence, that I am more of a Black man than all of you put together. Which one of you has ever travelled to, or ever lived in any African country? What do you really know about Africa or your African brothers and sisters? Exactly how much do you know about slavery and the slave trade, except what you heard from adults around you and all that crap you were fed in high school and college? Well, guys, I've got news for you. Except for the color of your skin, many of you are as White in orientation as your average White neighbor compared to the average African.

"Even when your African brothers and sisters come over to this country, you don't even get along. You laugh at them and consider them inferior to you. If that is not prejudice towards people of the same skin color and origin as you, I don't know what else to call it. If you care to ask, many of them will tell you that they get better reception and treatment from the average White guy than from African Americans of the same color and heritage. And, without a doubt, my father and other White people have done more for the development and well-being of the Black community here in America and in Africa than any African Americans can ever boast of or imagine.

"Do you know what is sad about this whole thing? Most of you do not even consider the fact or possibility that you may even be related by blood to most of these immigrants or visitors from Africa. There is a great chance that you have likely walked past, interacted with, or looked down upon, a long-lost cousin or relative every time you run into African immigrants or visitors.

"Must all Africans be the sons and daughters of slaves before you can accept them as your brothers and sisters?

Does the "African-American" classification now serve to distinguish a new 'race' of Blacks that are bound by descent or heritage from only those who were formerly slaves in America? Or, is it really a 'collective statement' that carries messages more profound than many people have bothered to think about? Some African Americans have expressed resentment towards Africans as interlopers – coming to reap benefits from where they did not sow sweat and blood.

"Guess what? A few details were obviously not included in the history books from which you were taught about slavery – particularly as it was practiced in Africa itself.

"Slaves were regarded as a special commercial "commodity" because there were various services that could be obtained from a variety of them almost free of charge. For those who were strictly slave dealers, though, captured slaves represented high risk and high maintenance costs if they could not find buyers for them. There were many factors that could have made a slave unattractive to potential buyers – illness, lack of space on board the vessels, or insufficient goods to purchase [since business was done by barter], and so on. Whatever the reason was, either of two things happened to slaves who didn't get sold to foreign or local slave buyers.

The "lucky" ones among the unsold slaves would have ended up being castrated and put to work in the Kings' Palaces, on various farms, and elsewhere. This meant a lifetime of hard labor with no remunerations, and no chance whatsoever of either experiencing the joys of sexual intercourse or producing any offspring."

According to Parsons, the unlucky ones who did not attract any buyers were eventually killed by their captors if they remained unsold for reasons ranging from physical defects to crippling illnesses, or kept to be used (killed) sometime in the future for ritualistic purposes. It wasn't good business for any captor to waste resources on a slave that could not attract buyers, or slaves that could not serve other useful purposes.

In those days when men of all colors and races were more of brutes, he said, it just didn't make economic sense for slave dealers to keep slaves who had very little or no prospect of bringing in any revenues. A slave had to earn his or her right to live through service, in whatever form the owner deemed it beneficial. Slaves that were deemed incapable of producing any sort of revenue or benefit were put down like sick animals.

Parsons asked if we were aware that specific numbers of slaves had to be killed and buried with major Traditional Rulers to continue to render service during the Ruler's journey in the afterlife. We were surprised to learn that these practices exist till this day in some African countries. I couldn't tell what the others were thinking, but everyone seemed captivated enough to let Parsons continue his ... lecture.

"In order to avoid the fate that awaited those who did not make it onto the slave ships, it is said that some slaves pleaded with potential slave buyers to be among those who would be bought and taken away. They were obviously prepared and willing to embrace the unknown rather than face the wickedness of ruthless local slave dealers and owners. There are yet unverified stories of what I like to describe as the occasional 'mercy purchases' during the era of the trans-Atlantic slave trade.

"This was the best term I could find to describe instances where slaves were bought by White men in response to some of the captives' pleas not to be separated from loved ones who had already been selected, or those who did not want to be left to face a grim future in the hands of local captors and slave owners. Wouldn't it be a great irony if some of the Blacks who demonize all White men and women are descendants of slaves who were 'grateful' to have been bought, and thus saved from a sealed fate?

"Till this day, Africans are still applying in throngs to foreign Embassies to flee their homelands into foreign territories they know little or nothing about, and whose cultures they are not familiar with. These Africans would rather live and feed on the least that is available from more humane White societies, than face indignity and poverty in homelands on a continent where human life seems to have very little or no value.

"You know what? The roles of slaves and slave-owners have swung back and forth like a pendulum between nations and communities over many thousands of years of human existence. There was a time in world history when powerful African nations (Egypt, for example) held citizens of other nations within and outside the continent in slavery. There would be no end to malice and bitterness if every nation and community held on to memories of humankind's acts of barbarism and inhumanity to one another.

"At the end of the day, it is about what people do with their lives once they got free from bondage of any sort. Many right-thinking nations and peoples who had suffered enslavement, at some point in history, continue to dedicate great resources towards implementing necessary laws and safeguards to ensure they never have to suffer the same fate again. A number of other nations and peoples have been lukewarm on the subject of stamping out slavery in any form that it still exists. For many unscrupulous business men and women worldwide, the business of human enslavement, for labor or sex among other services, is too lucrative to give up.

"It is unfortunate that the same fate that befell our Black ancestors (being forced into captivity and sold to the highest bidders) still befall many men, women and children in Africa till this day. At the time, the vile act of slave trading was successful only because of the participation of local authorities in connivance with unscrupulous individuals. The vile act continues to be successful even in these modern times in Africa for the same reasons. What is anyone saying or doing about that?

"It's not about being angry, guys. And, it's not so much about the White man as it is about re-shaping the perspectives of Blacks in this country, in particular, and in other parts of the world. In truth, if a number of the slaves who were taken out of Africa to the West and the Middle East had the opportunity, they would probably have sold or owned other people's brothers and sisters as slaves too.

"As a matter of historical fact, when tribes were conquered in battle, defeated chieftains and dignitaries who were once slave-owners or dealers often became slaves themselves. There is a great possibility that some of the slaves, who were bought in Africa and brought into this country by White slave traders, might have owned slaves in their homelands at some point in time.

"The capturing of vulnerable people for sale was simply standard business practice, and definitely one of the most lucrative businesses of the time. Look at what is happening now. Blacks are still killing and selling their own brothers and sisters right here, in broad daylight, in America and in Africa. Why has Black mentality, worldwide, remained mostly unchanged? Or, is it just something in the genes of Black folk?"

Obviously offended by Parsons' last remark, both Athiel and Kareem said they had heard just about enough. The Mulatto captive ignored them and simply continued his tirade. "Has it occurred to the leaders and members of the Black community in America that there just might be certain fundamental principles that providence led you here to learn, in order to lead and lift the Black race out of the darkness that threatens to consume it?

"As terrible as you say White people are, generally speaking, they continually demonstrate a preparedness to confront and overcome past and present demons, whether as a nation or as individuals, in order to try and improve past actions and practices that demeaned humanity. That much, unfortunately, cannot be said of Black people, generally speaking also. Has the Black race identified its demons in order to be able to confront and overcome them?"

"Are you done speaking now?" Athiel asked.

"I will only be done speaking when there's no longer any breath in me. Every day, I see more clearly why my late Uncle refused to back down from certain so-called inflammatory comments," said Parsons slowly, more to himself than anyone in particular. "To him, the comments were mere observations, which could easily have been addressed through healthy debates and the presentation of facts, if any, to prove the contrary. If it is your opinion that my views are wrong, then please educate me so that I can learn. What you have done to me serves no useful purpose in solving the problems of race in our society. Except for the thrill you got from committing this crime, there is nothing smart in what you guys have done. Right now, you are really killing me, and you don't even know it."

CHAPTER SIX

WHEN THOUGHTS TAKE FLIGHT

The entire episode with Parsons had gotten out of hand, particularly now that he could positively identify Ali Johnson, and possibly Kareem. None of this made any sense at all and, in some strange kind of way, I felt responsible for the entire fiasco.

By expressing a rather wild thought that I dismissed almost as quickly as it occurred to me, I had planted a bad seed in Kareem's mind. To see that wild and ridiculous notion played out in reality like this was nothing short of madness. Let me go back a little bit to give you some inkling about how a random thought, taken literally, had degenerated into a situation that could destroy all our lives.

Sometime after the Parsons' book promotion event from which Kareem stormed out, I had made a casual remark at one of our meetings to the effect that Parsons would not feel so smug if he really knew what it felt like to be a slave in those ignominious days. Kareem, who always got angry whenever Parsons' name came into the conversation, looked at me and smiled mischievously. It always bothered me whenever he had that look. You could never tell what he was going to do next.

If we could get Mr. President (Athiel, that was) to cooperate, Kareem had suggested, maybe it could be arranged for Parsons to experience what it was like to be a slave. Without attaching any kind of seriousness to the comment, many of the members laughed and one or two of them said that the idea would even be greater if it could be arranged for known White supremacists.

Athiel did not appear enthusiastic about the idea. At the time, I concluded that he was probably not quite as offended by Parsons' opinions as Kareem and a few other members of MBSK were. He politely suggested that Kareem should forget the frivolous idea, and encouraged him to be a little more tolerant in his views.

It has become to me that the idea was obviously not as frivolous as Athiel had described it, and that Kareem and these other guys had gone to great lengths to hatch and execute a sick plan. What I found incredible was Tanya's involvement and active role in such a daring but hare-brained scheme.

As I gathered much later, Kareem had convinced her to team up with him, Ali and Mo to teach Thomas Parsons a lesson he would never forget. Knowing how smitten Athiel was with his gorgeous and charming fiancée, I guess that was Kareem's way of ensuring Athiel's full cooperation and participation. Together, they stalked Parsons for about one week, and came up with a plan of action which included his kidnapping and the location that would be best suited for their mindless scheme.

After witnessing him 'at work' with Parsons, I promptly dismissed Athiel's claim that he participated only because he felt compelled to dig everybody out of the mess they had started. He would have me believe that he was so displeased with Tanya being an accomplice of the trio of Kareem, Ali Johnson and Mo Harvey in the kidnapping of an innocent man. Once the deed was done, he said, and with Tanya's neck-deep involvement, he had no other choice at the time than to go along with Kareem's plan to make Parsons' experience the suffering and evil of slavery.

Much later after I busted their sick scheme, I persuaded Kareem to give me details of the drug used by Athiel to induce the kind of hypnosis that made Parsons believe he was a slave. This information was required more for medical reasons than merely to satisfy my curiosity. It was of extreme importance to know how to counteract the effects of any drugs or chemical that had been introduced into his body.

Scopolamine – that was the name of the drug used by Athiel. In the early 50s, it was reported that Scopolamine was used as an interrogation drug by the CIA in covert mind-control and chemical interrogation research programs. Apart from being known as one of the popular types of truth serum, it was also known as a 'zombie' drug. In specified doses, Scopolamine is also used for medicinal purposes, particularly for symptoms of motion sickness. The drug could cause death if applied to the same person in large doses within a short period of time.

Two questions immediately popped into my head. First question: Why did Athiel need to carry around a significant quantity of a controlled substance like Scopolamine (classified as an evil mind-control drug when administered in high doses)? Second question: Where did he previously learn how to apply the drug to produce precise effects? Kareem later confessed that he was also quite surprised at Athiel's mastery of 'the game' of mind control. I had a vivid recollection of Athiel being in-charge and clearly loving the fact that he had a specimen on which to try out his silly drugs and experiments. Anyway, all of that nonsense didn't matter anymore.

So, back to the Kangaroo court convened by "judge" Athiel and company.

Tanya looked at me from the table and made a head gesture in Parsons' direction. I followed her gaze and noticed that Parsons was sweating profusely and hyperventilating. That was when I stepped out of the kitchen corridor into the utterly ridiculous setting that appeared more like an 'inquisition'. It was all too surreal for me.

"This needs to stop right now, guys. Are you guys completely out of your minds? You need to let this guy go, right now," I said very firmly, moving towards the table to appeal to Athiel and Kareem. I had no doubt they had all taken leave of their minds. Mo Harvey and Ali Johnson, I had always maintained, were a few cards short of a full deck. Anyway, that was it for me. I had seen and heard more than enough.

Parsons joined me in pleading for his own release, with the promise that he would not report the incident to law enforcement authorities. I added the fact that Parsons was not in good shape at all. Ali laughed and asked when I became a doctor. Athiel confirmed that Parsons didn't look like he was in good shape at all. He went closer to ask Parsons if he had ever been diagnosed with a cardiac problem. When Parsons answered in the affirmative and revealed that he was on prescription drugs, you could see the worry on Athiel's face. "This is not good," he muttered under his breath. "We need to get this man to a hospital."

When Mo protested vehemently against letting Parsons go because he had seen his face, it was clear that Kareem, Athiel, and Tanya had a problem they had not bargained for. It was clear to me that we needed to make a decision and act fast before Ali and Mo made us all accessories to murder. Parsons swore that he would not breathe or say a word to anybody. By that time, of course, my next move was perfectly clear in my head. I suggested that we should all go and grab a bite at a nearby Deli to discuss further and quickly too. To my relief, they all agreed. So, after securing Parsons in the basement, we got into our separate vehicles and drove behind Kareem, Tanya and Athiel as we headed for the neighborhood Deli that had become their local hang-out.

We had barely sat down when I told my friends that I needed to make a quick phone call. They pointed me in the direction of the payphone, situated in the access that led to the restrooms. About ten minutes later, literally stone-faced, I went back to the table and announced that the cops and an ambulance were on their way to the property to rescue Parsons. I told the guys that I had reported both a hostage situation and a medical emergency, and given the police information which they confirmed from the missing persons' report.

Kareem, Athiel, Tanya, Mo and Ali looked at me in disbelief, mouths agape. I glanced at my watch and told them that they probably had no more than ten minutes to clear any traces of their activities in that building before the cops arrive. "Don't worry guys. I told the police I got the tip from an anonymous caller. Just untie Parsons and leave him in there," I said. "And, seriously speaking, if I were you, I would move right now."

And, without any pleasantries, I turned and walked towards the Deli exit. "Where are you going, Carl?" Tanya asked. "I need to get out of this neighborhood, Tanya" I responded without looking back. Before I made it to the exit, my friends scurried past me, ran to their cars and sped off. You didn't need to be a rocket scientist to figure out where they were headed.

Of course I didn't call the cops or anyone. That would have been a very ill-advised move, and we would all have ended up in jail for a very long time. Really, I deserved an

Oscar for that performance. I did make a call to one of the Police Precincts downtown, but it was to follow up on a different matter with one of the officers. That was done in the event that one of those 'wise guys' decided to redial the last number I called if they didn't believe me. After the cop hung up, I stayed on the phone much longer having a conversation regarding Parsons' situation with no one but myself, just in case any one of them was trying to listen-in on my phone call.

I gave the guys a couple of minutes, and then drove to the same semi-concealed spot I had parked earlier to observe the building in which Parsons was held. When I was sure that Kareem, Athiel, Tanya, Mo and Ali had left the scene for good, I drove up to the property, picked Thomas Parsons up, and took him to a hospital of his choice somewhere downtown. From all accounts, it was a good thing we got him into the Emergency Room when we did.

Surprisingly, Parsons kept his word not to report the incident to law enforcement authorities. But, it was not easy for him to convince the doctors about how Scopolamine got into his system. In any case, Kareem, Athiel, Tanya, Mo and Ali were not taking any chances. Kareem, Athiel and Tanya flew out of the country for a long while, but still kept in touch with me (Kareem and Tanya more than Athiel).

On many occasions, I tried to assure them that Parsons was doing fine and had not entertained any thoughts of reporting the incident. I was convinced that Kareem and Tanya really felt bad about the Parsons' episode, but I will still bet money on the fact that Athiel had no regrets for having a subject like Parsons on which to practice his mind games. Kareem sent me recordings of what he described as a few interesting sessions with Parsons, admitting that his perspectives on slavery and race related issues actually did not sound as offensive as they did initially. Apparently, this was after he had taken time to digest his views.

The other two members of the 'abduction crew', Mo and Ali, literally disappeared from the face of the earth. As a matter of fact, I never really saw those two again, even though I cannot say that I did not 'hear' from them – loud and very clear.

When Parsons was discharged from the hospital immediately after the incident, we spent a lot of time together getting to know each other better – life perspectives and all. I couldn't stop apologizing for my friends and thanking him for honoring his word not to report the 'unforgettable' episode. Parsons, on the other hand, could not stop thanking me for taking a stand that prevented further torment and ultimately saved his life.

Parsons confessed that he had been trying very hard to forget some of the scenes that were now deeply etched into his mind during the ordeal. On one occasion, he recalled, it was as though he was being guided out of a subterranean prison and up a wooden stairway to the door of a large room filled with about a dozen men. There was an open fire pit in one corner of the room on which were some metal skewers and branding irons. By the side of open pit-fire, about six feet apart, were two young Black men. One of them was strapped to a sturdy-looking chair, while the other one was tied face down and butt-naked around a barrel supported by wooden stands.

While the others watched, the man in the chair had his lips pulled out for piercing with the red-hot skewers. And, like they do with horses and cattle, the other young Black man was being permanently marked as hot branding irons were pressed against his right butt-cheek. It was not difficult to see that they were sweating profusely and screaming. Even though I was given the mental picture of the young men's lips and butt-cheek sizzling, I could only imagine how loudly they must have been screaming from the horror on their faces.

Why on earth did I need to be made to see or imagine such unspeakable horror? There are certain things in this world that are better left to the imagination, and this scene was one of them.

According to Parsons, he started gaining a notion that nothing he had experienced was real only about two days before I came onto the scene. "Here, Mr. Parsons," he said he heard a deep but gentle voice say, as two keys were thrown to the ground beside him from the doorway to the cellar. "Unlock the padlocks on your ankles. Let us get this over with as quickly as possible."

Parsons said he would probably have been overjoyed at the sound of that voice if only his heart would stop pounding like it was going to explode in his chest. What was there to get over with as quickly as possible, he thought – his last day on earth or what? He said that he was especially curious to know who was behind the whole thing.

As he unlocked the ankle clamps, heart still pounding, he heard the same voice say gently again, "If you are worried, Mr. Parsons, there's no need to be." He was told that he would be appearing in front of a 'jury' of his peers, but he needed a shower and a good meal first." The reference to a shower, as Parsons saw it, gave him some hope. After all, you didn't need to be clean to be killed.

The lights, he said, hurt his eyes as he was ushered up the cellar stairway to the living room above. Parsons recalled being reminded by a rather menacing voice that it was okay to stand up straight to walk. His brain had been deceived for an extended period of time into thinking he was in some type of subterranean dwelling where he had to crouch at all times. Parsons later matched that voice to the face he positively identified later – Mo Harvey. During his first encounter with his captors, he noted that all the men were dark skinned, and wearing Western clothing – from jeans and T-shirts to sport coats.

Parsons was guided to a bathroom where there were two buckets filled with water, a little bowl floating in one of the buckets, a sponge and a bar of soap. In another corner of the room, he noted there was a pair of new boxer shorts, a t-shirt and a towel piled on top of a high wooden stool. All these signs, he said, were quite encouraging. After all, you don't dress a turkey up and then kill it; you kill it first and dress it up later.

On the floor near the stool was a disposable cup with a cheap toothbrush, carrying a dab of toothpaste, lying across its rim. There was no hot water, but he said that he quickly got used to it, adding that mere words could not describe how exhilarating that particular shower was.

Afterwards, he was shown into the sparsely furnished living room in which there was a medium sized table with four chairs. Even before he entered the room, he told me, the smell of delicious food had wafted down the corridor as they approached. Two eggs sunny side up, two strips of bacon and two sausages with two pancakes, and a steaming hot cup of coffee. "Lord have mercy, I thought and half-smiled. The joy of knowing that I was still in America made the meal even more appealing. This was America alright," Parsons said. "I would recognize a hearty IHOP breakfast any day, anytime."

CHAPTER SEVEN

SELFLESSNESS AND SELFISHNESS

A question by a reporter, during a public speaking event, exposed Thomas Parsons and his uncle, Late Congressman Buttons, as sharing the opinion that White people are better than Black people.

How, and in what ways, could anyone have come to that determination? It's no wonder the Late Congressman was considered racist by many. Did he think that White people were better than Black people intellectually, in looks and physical attributes, in moral standing, or simply inferior as human beings as they used to believe? Parsons' admission that he shared that opinion also, more than anything else he said, almost got him mobbed by some very angry Black dudes after the speaking event.

This was an issue I had wanted to bring up with him for quite a while, but had to hold back because of his serious and unstable health condition. On that particular day, he was up and perky – just the right kind of mood in which I had been hoping to catch him. So, during one of my almost-now-routine trips to the hospital to check on his health, I looked straight into his eyes as I asked if he really felt that way, and why.

"That was a generalization," he clarified, looking back at me with a coy smile. "You didn't forget that comment, huh?" he asked. I responded by shaking my head, and he added "And you want to know how we came to that conclusion, right?" "Uh huh," I answered and also nodded in response to his question.

In support of his comment that White people are better than Black people, I reminded him that he had used the word 'selfish' to describe Black people, while describing White people as 'selfless'.

Stating my points as calmly and as firmly as I could without raising my voice, I tried to emphasize the existence of evidence that the White race has perpetuated a campaign of extreme selfishness across the globe. It is clear, even in their international policies and practices, that White nations are concerned primarily with their own interests and welfare, with little or no regard for others. The White race went into Africa and some other parts of the world, supposedly under a divine obligation to bring the locals out of a primitive existence into civilization.

As it turned out, nothing mattered more to these 'White would-be do-gooders' than being well positioned to plunder the communities they were pretending to help. Compared to the enormous wealth acquired from exploiting less developed nations around the world, what could one say that the White colonial masters gave back to those nations and their peoples? How else would you characterize such a history, Parsons?

Parsons nodded in agreement, which was rather surprising. He wanted me to realize, though, that every living organism has an in-built trait of selfishness; that is, a desire to seek and ensure 'personal' survival or self-preservation in any way, and by any means, possible. According to Parsons, the most important words to note here are 'personal' and 'self-preservation', and how human beings, in particular, give expression to them.

Although seriously limited at the early stages of human existence, the understanding and interpretation of 'personal' and 'self' have evolved considerably, with individuals and as groups, according to our different levels of consciousness or spiritual maturity. For so many, at some point in time, these words translated to what we now describe as 'me, myself, and I' and nobody else (an attitude that is still prevalent in our communities).

To others, 'personal' and 'self' meant matters relating, or pertaining, to a particular individual. The scope or sphere covered by this interpretation, or the understanding of it, has varied quite significantly over the years – from the immediate family to close relatives, or to people of the same race, ethnicity, color, and religious persuasion, or to geographical locations, the entire human race, and even our earthly environment.

At the end of the day, it is important that we all come to the realization that what happens to every human being and our earthly environment relates or pertains to us on a 'personal' level. The welfare of the human race and this earth is about your 'self'.

When you help or perform an act of goodness to someone else, you help so many other people than you could possibly imagine, and you help yourself also. If you perpetrate evil to undermine anybody, you would be undermining and hurting more human beings than you care to imagine, and you ultimately are hurting and undermining yourself. When you pollute or tamper recklessly with the earth, you endanger others including yourself.

In short, Parsons said, selfishness actually begins to end only when the definition and understanding of what constitutes an individual's personal interest becomes broadened in scope. This, he said, is an indicator that shows how much a person is becoming 'one' with his or her fellow human beings, and the world as a whole. With regards to the expansionist programs and policies of the Western nations over hundreds of years, he agreed that they did demonstrate a primary concern or interest in the collective welfare of their societies above all others.

"Thanks for the lecture and the long grammar, but what was the problem with how I phrased it and what you just said?" I asked.

The problem, he said, was this: That was a long, long time ago when every community's definition of 'personal interest' ranged from narrow to extremely narrow. For many White people, the definition and understanding of 'personal interest' and 'self' has since broadened significantly to include the global human family and how we deploy our planet's resources. That is the direction where we all need to be headed.

These days, he stated, some human beings just seem to have evolved in the definition of what self-preservation is, to the point where they harbor a greater level of preparedness to sacrifice personal gains for the benefit and advancement of others. That preparedness to sacrifice, and how narrowly or broadly each one of us defines the membership of our immediate 'family', determines how selfish or selfless we are as human beings. The truth, in recent times, is that more Whites than Blacks have demonstrated a greater level of preparedness to sacrifice personal gains, comforts, and interests for the collective benefit and advancement of the global human family."

"That," I said, "did not remove the fact that their actions either damaged or seriously complicated systems that needed to evolve naturally, and at their own pace. The point is that Western nations went into those undeveloped nations with the sole aim of plundering, and most definitely not for humanitarian reasons as they would like to claim. They plundered those nations of both human and natural resources for personal and national benefits. Looking at the foreign policy of this nation and its Western counterparts, nothing has changed. I find it difficult to imagine what the basis could be for anyone to come to the determination that White people are better than Black people. At least, generally speaking also, Black people are not hypocrites like White people are."

"I don't know about that, but I hear you, Carl. In those days, many nations exploited one another because they knew no better. Yes, the strong took advantage of the weak. From our perspective in present times it was wrong, but this has been the story of mankind for many thousands of years until recent times. By the way, Carl, leaders of formerly White-ruled African colonies have inflicted more serious damage to their nations and committed unthinkable atrocities since achieving independent rule."

Comparing the current state of affairs of these former colonies, he said, it is almost as clear as daylight that the Colonialists had more regard for the welfare and development of those nations than do the locals who have been in governance since the Colonialists departed. Ironically, former Colonialist nations still extend many courtesies to citizens of their former colonies as a moral obligation to ensure the collective welfare, as opposed to their current governments. This is more than you can say for their leaders, who show no moral obligation whatsoever for the welfare and development of their own people and countries.

However, he continued, what constitutes the major difference between Whites and Blacks is the inclusiveness of the broadened scope of survival and self-preservation of White people. With Black people, 'personal' interests and welfare relate or pertain to an individual and the immediate family – not even the larger community of fellow Blacks with which they have a lot in common. He added that this was notwithstanding the fact that all human beings have much more in common than not.

In Parsons' opinion, even though all races and cultures in the past can be criticized for their less than noble definitions of what represented personal interests in this world, they still found commonality in their economic and imperial expansionist policies. Till this day, the Black community is yet to embrace all members of its own race as one family, for which it should seek to advance, promote, and protect its interests and welfare.

He argued that the deeper concepts of 'family' and 'support' are not visible enough in the way that Blacks relate with one another, or care for themselves as a family, much less others. "Hey, Carl, does it not appear to you that most Blacks, in different parts of the world, feel that the only way to survive is to feed off, and destroy, each other? Like crabs in a bucket, I have observed what has become a tradition of many Black people to pull down and trample on other Blacks to prevent them from getting to the top. The support system is weak for the average Black even within his or her own community. This pattern of behavior is not as common among Whites as it is among Blacks."

Parsons suggested that the Black community in this country, and throughout the world, needs to work towards finding cohesion. Also, he said, the Black community is yet to grasp the depth of the vision of Dr. Martin Luther King Jr. that they must rise above being just a color to become part of 'one' human race with unimaginable potential. The truth is that Blacks are not doing enough to harness, defend and promote their substantial collective resources, and nobody can do it for them but themselves.

"Are these the only reasons you have to support your point of view that Whites are better than Blacks?" I asked, wondering what else he had to add in support of his out-landish opinion.

"There are many more reasons, Carl. For instance, I can boldly say, and I always do, that a greater percentage of Whites see beyond race and color than an equal per-centage of Blacks. Tell me, Carl, how many times do you see Black people coming out to support or champion a 'cause' for Whites or any other race? On the other hand, I cannot count how many times White folks and other non-Blacks have joined hands to support or champion Black causes."

"From what you told me, Parsons, your experience in Africa was wonderful and filled with fond memories," I interjected. He answered in the affirmative and wanted to know where I was going with that statement. "While I am aware that your mother was a Black woman, your comments and general attitude towards Black people and Black issues can easily be construed to mean that you do not see anything good in Black people. Going by the kind of statements you make, Parsons, the whole world might as well be White. You know ... get-rid-of-Black-people-and-the-world-would-be-a-better-place sort of thing."

He smiled and took a long look at me. "That's not correct, Carl. On the contrary, it's just that I see a lot of potential in the Black man, and the entire race, that is being squandered on hate-mongering. Look at you, a decent, smart and principled young Black man. I know for a fact that there are so many more like you out there – in different parts of the world. My concern is that so many Black men and women are not aware of the depth of their potentials, and the value they can add to their own lives and the advancement of the human race.

"At the same time also, I know that the world is yet to find out just how much the Black race can 'bring to the global table'. I know Black people in ways that White people cannot ever know them. Conversely, I know White people in so many other ways than Black people think they know them. As things are in the world today, I can say with a high degree of certainty that Black people, generally speaking, are holding back on giving their best to the world. Or, better still, something seems to be holding them back from addressing issues that can propel the race to the greatest heights in all fields of human endeavor. What could the problem be? I really cannot put a finger on what the problem is, and there lies my frustration with those who are a part of me – my being.

"Just like most of our ancestors, Black people are mostly brave and courageous, kind, warm and hospitable, long-suffering and slow to anger. Of course, some were just as evil as members of any race could ever have been. History, from the African perspective, shows Black heritage as consisting of many proud but warm-hearted ancestors, whose communities were operated on a system of noble codes of honor and ethics. Their word was their bond, and they were reputed to be willing to give up their lives to protect trust and confidence reposed in them. Unfortunately, those qualities also made them extremely vulnerable to charlatans.

"African tradition and history reveals that betrayal – in any form or manner, and probably more than anything else – has always represented a 'sticking point' for the Black psyche.

"Call it whatever you will – abuse of trust, 'playing a person for the fool', repaying kindness with evil – acts of betrayal seem to cause a kind of profound hurt that the Black psyche appears to have difficulty overcoming. And, while they may be willing to make peace just to move on, one could characterize them as unforgiving because they are not likely to let you (or themselves) ever forget. Is this a good thing? I do not think so.

"African history shows that Black ancestors were quick to trust and happy to share, while expecting those 'worthy' of being addressed as human beings to be guided in their thinking and actions by some degree of honor and ethics.

"I am almost convinced that the psyche of the African-American, in particular, has gone into basic survival mode – 'trust no one but suspect everyone, and look out for yourself because no one else will or cares'. This is a protective mode that probably arose from repeated hurt and betrayal. One of the ways in which the condition manifests is 'indifference' – a negative attitude that, more often than not, spells disaster for all. When one, as an individual or group, becomes indifferent to the plight of all others except one's own, the only word that best describes that kind of attitude is ... selfishness. In the same vein, when one becomes indifferent to kindness or sacrifices made on one's behalf, that shows nothing but ingratitude. At the end of the day, selfishness and ingratitude make a person more loathsome that those he or she loathes."

What he said made a lot of sense, and I just sat there by his bedside trying to digest every point he had made. "I hope you now see where I am coming from." he said, the sound of his voice interrupting that brief but poignant moment. "Maybe I am a dreamer, Carl, or maybe I just fell in love with the way my dad used to preach the story of Joseph, the son of Jacob, in the biblical Book of Genesis. There was something about the story that rang true with the saga of the African who was sold by his own brothers into slavery and taken to a foreign land where he eventually prospered."

CHAPTER EIGHT

JOSEPH AND THE AFRICAN-AMERICAN SLAVE

According to Thomas Parsons:

Without a doubt, current African-American leaders are yet to recognize that they have a higher calling in this world. As such, they are failing in the fulfillment of this higher calling. I am close to drawing the conclusion that most African-Americans, the leaders in particular, have really not considered the role that providence might have played in the torturous journey of their ancestors from Africa to the most powerful nation on earth. What I am getting ready to say, however, applies in some degree to all Blacks whose ancestors also journeyed from slavery to membership of some of the most advanced nations in the world. To me, there was a greater purpose behind that fateful journey into the 'unknown'.

I am convinced that they were led out of Africa by providence to raise a new breed of Black men and women who would become worthy of partaking in, and contributing to, decisions that will ultimately affect the course of human affairs, of which their race must play a vital part. It is with regards to this higher mandate I believe that Black leaders, African-Americans in particular, are failing. For them not to miss the bigger picture, as most of us often do, it will be important that they are able to see beyond "self".

Firstly, many people all over the globe have come to accept the fact that the dynamics behind where each human being is born on earth, and also under what circumstances and in what color, is still beyond our understanding and control. Secondly, sometimes we are born at our ultimate destination on earth, and sometimes we are born at a location very far from where we eventually end our journey in life.

Regarding the latter, however, that final destination on earth may not always necessarily be of our choosing initially. That final destination may be where providence leads us, hard and winding as the road may be.

For the right thinking man or woman, therefore, surely the slowly unfolding events in life have to be a whole lot more than a mere game of chance or coincidence. It is for this reason that many have spent entire lifetimes trying to determine... purpose. With the benefit of hindsight, some degree of good seems to have emerged from the 'ashes' of many events that were once considered 'extremely unfortunate' in our history of development. The eventual beneficial outcomes to human societies, many have suggested, can be attributed to providence.

In the Holy Bible [Genesis Chapters 39-50], for example, Joseph the son of Isaac was born in Canaan, a former historical region in what is now referred to as the Middle East. Even though he was born into a family of great wealth and influence, he was said to have been sold to foreigners as a slave by his own brothers. It is important to note that he was not sold into slavery for his weakness, but for his strength – his God-given asset.

In what many might regard today as a 'twist of fate', Joseph eventually became Governor of the nation of Egypt when it was at its most powerful. As Governor, he was second in rank and power to the Pharaoh, despite being listed among peoples that Egyptians found "detestable" – Hebrews. His change of fortune can be attributed to the fact that he did not allow his spirit to be broken and consumed by the horrors and humiliation of captivity. He honed his asset – his strength – and made himself relevant to his captors and the Egyptian community. From the dungeons of captivity, Joseph was elevated to the exalted position of Governor of Egypt. In this new capacity, he was able to add value to the lives of all and sundry – particularly those of his kinfolk who had sold him into slavery in the first place.

Just like the Biblical Joseph, the 'African-American', metaphorically speaking, was initially captured and betrayed by his own brothers, and sold as a slave to foreigners long ago. He, also, like Joseph, was offered for sale and bought on account of the strength of his assets, and definitely not because of his weakness. And, just like Joseph's brothers, those who sold him have lied and pretended that they played no part in what became of their own brother. Today, that free man who became a slave is not only free again, but he has now become a Prince — elevated way above many of his fellowmen, particularly the brothers who betrayed and sold him into slavery.

From the chains, the padlocks and the stench of the dungeons, he found favor with God and his captors and has risen to become a stakeholder and partaker at the pinnacle of world governance and power in the most powerful nation on the face of the earth. This is not coincidence at all. Coincidence, it has been said, is a word that was coined to enshroud the general lack of understanding of how events in the lives of men and women are determined.

A traditional African prayer of parents for their children is this: May God bless your worthy endeavors, enrich your life to be better than ours, and enable you to surpass us in achievement. Probably more than anything else, the prayer of the ancestors of African-Americans has been answered. At this point in time in history, the lives of Blacks who have been assimilated into Western society have been enriched, their worthy endeavors have been blessed, and they have definitely surpassed their ancestors in achievement.

To my mind, every slave taken out of Africa was 'a Joseph'. By being citizens of powerful nations around the world, every one of them has become a Prince or Princess compared to their brothers and sisters in their original homelands. Also, just like Joseph's former homeland became desolate, the homelands out of which Blacks were sold are becoming "desolate" of hope, opportunities and humanity. Those who sold them into slavery have now come clamoring to the nations to which they sold their brothers and sisters in search of hope, opportunities and a better way of life. By the grace of God, their brothers and sisters have become Princes and Princesses in those great nations.

There is another parallel which can be drawn from the events that unfolded between the Biblical Joseph and his brothers, and the African-American and his brothers from Africa. Unfortunately, however, the outcome of the eventual encounter between the Biblical and African American slaves who became Princes and the brothers who sold them into slavery was so many 'poles apart'.

The Biblical Joseph who was betrayed and sold into slavery took the higher road, in attitude and approach, which set his brothers and their descendants on the path of relevance and greatness. The African (now African American) who rose from slave to Prince, on the other hand, adopted an attitude and approach that has led his brothers and their descendants down the road of unending conflict and destitution. That lesser road has left the brothers and sisters and relatives of the African-American "hungry and waiting to be fed" just about anything from unscrupulous people who peddle false hopes and opportunities.

Regardless of Joseph's personal pain and grievance, he remained just as concerned about the integrity and continued survival of his immediate family as he was about all other within his sphere of influence. Joseph sought to ensure that hunger and poverty would not drive his family to the point of having to undermine their heritage and values.

For Black people generally, it is most unfortunate that poverty, even in the midst of plenty, continues to serve as the biggest contributive factor to the gradual loss of heritage and values.

It says in the Biblical story of Joseph thus:

…Then Judah went up to him and said: "Please, my lord, let your servant speak a word to my lord. Do not be angry with your servant, though you are equal to Pharaoh himself. My lord asked his servants, 'Do you have a father or a brother?' And we answered, 'We have an aged father, and there is a young son born to him in his old age. His brother is dead, and he is the only one of his mother's sons left, and his father loves him.' "Then you said to your servants, 'Bring him down to me so I can see him for myself.' [Genesis 44:18-22]

Within these verses are very pertinent points. The first is that Joseph's brothers and parents had fulfilled the prophetic dream that was interpreted to mean that his parents and brothers would eventually bow to him in deference. Joseph's prophecy has been fulfilled in the saga of how providence led the African slave into relevance and honor in the greatest nation on earth. The second pertinent point is that Joseph had requested to see their most junior brother, Benjamin, to ascertain that the young man had not suffered a terrible fate in the hands of his older siblings, just as he (Joseph) did.

African-Americans, in particular, have been raised above all the rest of their brethren in Africa. African-Americans have become almost everything that their brothers and sisters in Africa aspire to be. They now hold sway in the 'courts' of the mightiest nation on earth, and have a say in the affairs of the rest of the world. But, when Africans throng the different US Embassies and finally succeed in gaining entry into the country to appease their hunger for opportunities, have African-Americans 'asked' them what has become of the 'last born' of the families left behind in Africa?

The story goes on to show us that Joseph's brothers had obviously grown more thoughtful and responsible by demonstrating a preparedness to sacrifice their freedom and personal ambitions to secure the safety and freedom of their most junior brother. Africans are yet to grow more caring and responsible for the general well-being and safety of their brothers and sisters. They are now probably worse than ever before. And, even though White colonialism is still being blamed for the displacement and fracturing of African communities, the 'dark' continent is really living up to its name in the perpetration of untold evil. While the Biblical Joseph demanded accountability before welcoming and providing security for former perpetrators of evil, African-Americans literally fold their arms, mostly preferring to wine and dine with those who continue to perpetrate the same old evil practices that have caused horror and pain for far too long.

It was when Joseph saw the positive change in attitude and thinking – the selflessness in particular – of those who previously had no compunction about his fate in the hands of foreign slave dealers that he found it difficult to hold back his true identity from his brothers. In other words, Joseph finally found release for what must have been a pent-up emotion; a release that enabled healing and reconciliation.

…"Have everyone leave my presence." So there was no one with Joseph when he made himself known to his brothers. And he wept so loudly that the Egyptians heard him, and Pharaoh's household heard about it. Joseph said to his brothers, "I am Joseph! Is my father still living?" But his brothers were not able to answer him, because they were terrified at his presence.

Then Joseph said to his brothers, "Come close to me." When they had done so, he said, "I am your brother Joseph, the one you sold into Egypt. And now, do not be distressed and do not be angry with yourselves for selling me here, because it was to save lives that God sent me ahead of you. …God sent me ahead of you to preserve for you a remnant on earth and to save your lives by a great deliverance.

"So then, it was not you who sent me here, but God. … You can see for yourselves, and so can my brother Benjamin, that it is really I who am speaking to you. Tell my father about all the honor accorded me in Egypt and about every-thing you have seen. And bring my father down here quickly."

Then he threw his arms around his brother Benjamin and wept, and Benjamin embraced him, weeping. And he kissed all his brothers and wept over them. Afterward his brothers talked with him. …Then he sent his brothers away, and as they were leaving he said to them, "Don't quarrel on the way!" …

The Biblical story of Joseph concludes with the death of his father (Isaac) and the fear of Joseph's brothers that they might suffer retaliation at the hands of the brother that they had treated so badly and sold into slavery.

…"What if Joseph holds a grudge against us and pays us back for all the wrongs we did to him?" So they sent a message to Joseph, saying, "Your father left these instruc-tions before he died: 'This is what you are to say to Joseph: I ask you to forgive your brothers the sins and the wrongs they committed in treating you so badly.' Now please for-give the sins of the servants of the God of your father." When their message came to him, Joseph wept.

His brothers then came and threw themselves down before him. "We are your slaves," they said.

But Joseph said to them, "Don't be afraid. Am I in the place of God? You intended to harm me, but God intended it for good to accomplish what is now being done, the saving of many lives. So then, don't be afraid. I will provide for you and your children." And he reassured them and spoke kindly to them…" [Genesis 50:15-21]

There is another important lesson to learn, among many others, from Joseph's story. The lesson is in how he named his first two sons. The meaning of the name of his first son, Manasseh, reflected the ways in which God had made him forget all his troubles and his father's household. In essence, Joseph had 'let go' of the horrors and pains of captivity, put the past behind him, and carved a new destiny for himself. He forgave everyone who had made his life hell on earth – his brothers, the slave buyers and the slave masters.

Joseph named his second Ephraim to capture, in meaning, his heartfelt gratitude to God for his success even in the land where he had suffered bitterly. After all, as we gather from the story, things could have been worse. He barely escaped the original intent of his brothers to kill him and he could have been left to rot in the dungeons for a crime he never committed.

In the end, it did not matter whether Joseph or the African was initially tied with ropes and placed in a pit by their own brothers to be sold into slavery, and later bound in chains and branded by foreign slave-owners, the fact is that providence has been on their side.

No one can be at peace with the world if he or she is not at peace with himself or herself, and with God.

To those who ask, there is nothing wrong with the Black man except that he must first heal and seek peace, first within himself and then within his 'immediate Black family'. Relating to the larger global human community, thereafter, will become much easier.

Great as providence may be, we must all learn that it is not without significant input from every man and woman.

I got back to the office after being in court all day and was informed by the receptionist that there was an urgent message waiting on my desk. The moment I saw Irene's name on it, my heart skipped a few beats. I knew it was not going to be good news at all, and I was right. Thomas Parsons' heart had failed and he had been rushed to the hospital.

Fearing the worst, and totally forgetting how exhausted I had been, I took off like a bat out of hell. I am not so sure I was as glad to see him all wired up in the Intensive Care Unit as he was to see me. But, thank goodness, he was still alive. Irene's normally calm demeanor had changed, and that said a lot – the situation was not good. Parsons was calm as usual, though. We spoke for a few minutes, and he handed me an envelope with a typed manuscript in it. "I know you will do it justice, Carl," he said, smiling.

"It's a good thing that I have come to understand you the way I do now," I told Parsons. "For many of us Black first-time attendees, your speeches were extremely provocative. Your perspectives about the Black community seemed to be driven by a desire to impress your White relatives at the expense of your Black relatives. We drew the conclusion, probably rather too quickly, that you had taken a side – the White side. If I were to be asked right now which side you were on, my answer would be quite different. But, did you have to be so provocative to make your point?"

Obviously weak and tired, and without looking at me, Parsons merely smiled and said, "Black people are generally too laid-back, my friend. I needed to make them angry enough to vent. Don't forget — African Americans are of the same gene pool as their brothers and sisters in the part of Africa from which most were brought here. They are long-suffering, and known to repress anger in the hope that things would change in the course of time without necessarily having to push too hard.

"The lives and fortunes of all men and women, they believe, are determined by supernatural forces. For them, to accept the dictates of life and exercise restraint is a demonstration of maturity and a submission to the higher authority of the Creator. In other words, many are likely to react only when 'pushed to the wall'. Black people have a tendency to allow 'things' to grow that could possibly have been nipped in the bud.

"This is one of those areas where the White mindset is vastly different. Unlike the average Black man, the average White man is constantly searching for ways to take control of the circumstances that determine the outcome of their lives and environment. The average White man does not believe that problems will just go away unless they are vigorously addressed or tackled. While change is difficult to effect or accept, they are prepared to put in the required effort — no matter how monumental — to achieve their goal.

"You know what, Carl? I pray that the day will come when a person's allegiance to humanity will be greater than allegiance to race, color and religion, or even flags. Maybe we need to set aside just one day in the calendar year as a day of reconciliation; a day for families, friends, communities and nations to try and heal old wounds. We need to try and find and restore whatever we all might have lost during the tumultuous but interesting human journey on this earth."

There I was, eyes clouding with tears, standing at the foot of the hospital bed watching life slowly ebb out of my friend. Irene was there by his side, as usual. She was rubbing his left shoulder, trying to smile, but she couldn't control the tears. Her nephew, my friend – yes, my friend – the Black White man, was on his way out for sure, and both of us knew that. Thomas Parsons was getting ready to exit the world stage. He thanked her and told her he would be fine. The doctors said that there was not much they could do for him again. With his kind of heart disease, the doctors said, the condition was almost certainly terminal. His ordeal at the hands of Athiel and the others had pushed his heart to the limit, and it was only a matter of time. His heart was just not pumping enough blood to sustain his life. The level of regurgitation in his right atrium was quite high. His legs and hands were swollen, and his glowing skin had darkened considerably.

"Isn't that something, Carl?" he said with a faint smile when he saw me looking at his exposed legs. "At the rate my skin color is changing, it seems like I am going to die

Black." Irene and I laughed, even though she was crying and I was already sniffling. I could not believe that Parsons was still cracking jokes at a time like that. "Don't worry, buddy. I'm not dying. The spirit does not die. I just need to go for a change of working tools – a new heart, liver, kidneys, hands and legs – and a new clothing of skin. Come over here and sit by me, Carl. I want to ask you something."

I pulled the chair as close as I could get to the bed, sat down, and he held my hand. "Tell me," he whispered, "have you ever seen an angel?"

No, I said in reply, and requested to know why he asked that question. To say that my heart was beating really fast would have been an understatement. "It all started whenever I fell asleep. There would be a flurry of activity around me involving very friendly strangers and people that I used to know – like, you know, my parents and or two people who had died long ago. It's all so nice and peaceful and every-thing, Carl, but I have not seen anyone with wings. These days, whether my eyes are close or not, Carl, I see these same beautiful friendly figures. Somehow, I know they are angels, but I just wanted to share something special with you. My mother and father, my brother, the different people I knew and all these angels are all the same color – no color at all. Can you beat that? All that fuss about color for absolutely nothing. I see no color here at all."

With tears slowly running down my face, I sensed that his time was drawing close. The welcoming committee was already there to ensure a smooth and pleasant passage.

"Come to think of it, Thomas" I said, calling him by his first name for the first time, "I did get to meet an angel here on earth. Guess most of us just never recognize them in good time. He was called the Black White man. How could I have known that angels had earthly names and nicknames? But, now I know. They work their magic and change lives in ways that we don't expect."

My speech was interrupted by the loud monotonous bleep of the heart monitor. Nurses and doctors rushed into the room and nobody needed to tell me to get out of the way. I looked at his face, peaceful and smiling, as I let go of his hand. Somehow, despite efforts that were made to try and revive him, I knew in my heart that Thomas Parsons – the Black White man – had come to the end of this segment of his journey on earth.

I was very happy that Kareem and Tanya had summoned the courage to visit Parsons the previous day. The visit was quite emotional, but Parsons tried hard to assure them they were already forgiven. Coming from Parsons, that was a very profound statement. Even though the guys always tried to skirt the subject of Parsons' steadily deteriorating condition, I seized every opportunity to let them realize their culpability for Parsons' dilemma.

Kareem and Tanya liked to argue that Parsons was already suffering from a life-threatening disease. While that was true, it was also true that his abduction and torture only served to exacerbate his poor medical condition. Parsons was prevented from taking prescribed daily mandatory medication for about a week, injected with higher-than-normal doses of dangerous mind-bending cocktails, and exposed to conditions tantamount to physical torture. No matter how short Parsons' life might have been on account of a pre-existing and mostly terminal illness, the actions of his abductions ensured it was even shorter. Legally speaking, Kareem, Athiel, Tanya, Mo and Ali were culpable, whichever way they wished to slice or dice.

Parsons was fully aware of this because the doctors expressed regret about his "decision" to stop taking the prescribed medication for such a prolonged period. It was not only unwise, the doctors had said, the carelessness had caused further damage to his heart that left almost no room for survival.

Thomas Parsons showed no bitterness towards Kareem and Tanya when they eventually showed up at the hospital, and expressed none towards the co-conspirators who were conspicuously absent. Tanya and Kareem accepted their guilt and begged for Parsons' forgiveness, which they got without much ado. In Parsons' last words to Tanya and Kareem, "Let's hope we all gained something from our joint experience."

CHAPTER NINE
THE DEBATE

The death of Thomas Parsons hit me in a way that I least expected, even though I had only known, and interacted with, him for less than a year. I guessed it must have been a combination of things, including guilt that my wild idea and the reckless actions of my friends had seriously interrupted and undermined his life. We had also developed a very special bond over that short period of time – as friends, brothers and working partners.

A couple of weeks after Parsons' death, I received a small package from the Middle East. I knew it had to be from Kareem Hamada, who had traveled back to the Middle East about a week after Parsons' funeral. Inside the package was a note signed by Kareem, stuck with a thin strip of tape to a Maxwell Chrome cassette tape in its casing. The note read:

"My brother, I just wanted to share a part of the infamous session with the Black White Man that I have played back so many times. I am so very sorry about your wife, Carl. We have a good idea who masterminded the attack.

You have my assurance; the deed will not go unpunished. Please remain as strong as you've always been, man. Hope to see you soon. Thanks and good luck."

When I got home later that evening, I popped the cassette into my little stereo set to get an idea of what Kareem was talking about. And, since I didn't know exactly how long the recording was, I got a beer to sip on, pressed the 'play' button, and stretched out on the sofa.

The following is a transcript, somewhat, of the debate Thomas Parsons and the Athiel-led group constituted by himself, Kareem, Tanya, Ali Johnson, and Mo Harvey. The transcription, in italics, is interspersed with my comments to provide some degree of clarity to a convoluted development. Obviously, Kareem had edited and cued the tape at the point he wished to share with me. The audio started with Parsons speaking:

"...Pardon me, it's just that I don't consider it politically correct to call you African-American any more than European or Asian immigrants should seek identity by their country of origin. German-Americans, Italian-Americans, British-Americans, African-Americans, naturalized American from different nations of the world — we are all Americans, right? It has never made much sense to me why Blacks in this country wish to be addressed as African-Americans. Anyway, that's neither here nor there."

It didn't sound as if Parsons was expecting an answer really, but no one said a word. So, I imagined, he continued. You could almost detect that his voice sounded tinged with a little bit of anger.

"...Slavery is over, guys. As evil and contemptuous as slavery was, it is over. As far as the United States of America is concerned anyway, it has been over for a long time. And, that's a fact. But guess who made this possible long before the great Martin Luther King Jr. was born? The same White folks that you love to condemn and blame for all your woes. It makes me so angry that we have a hypocritical Black community that refuses to acknowledge the fact that freedom from slavery and subsequent advancement was advanced and supported by White folks. However, bad some White people may have been (or still are), a greater number of them were, and are still, decent and God-fearing people. Yes. White folks were decent enough to confront the evil of ownership and enslavement of men by their fellow men. That, unfortunately, cannot be said of your relatives in Africa who sold their own people in the first place and still continue to do so, or hold them in some form of bondage or the other."

A female voice which I knew to be Tanya's chimed in:

"Wow, it appears we have here a man who is embittered with the fact that he has Black blood mixed with the precious White blood that's flowing through his veins. I don't think your mother will be very proud of you for running her people down all the time. Very soon you will be exposed for who you really are — a racist and a bigot?"

Parsons responded:

"If you waited to read my book without already forming opinions on it, you might have found out that I was actually advancing a case for solutions to race issues, which affects Blacks more than any other issues in this country. And, unless someone convinces me otherwise, I do not believe that the enormous potentials of the Black community in this country will ever be achieved by a continued expectation of government to provide 'crutches and wheelchairs' for healthy men and women."

Tanya came in once again:

"That's right. I almost forgot about that. You did liken affirmative action to crutches and wheelchairs, Mr. Parsons. That was an ignorant thing to say. After all we've been through, nothing would be better for Blacks in this country — at least for a start. Now that women have been added via Executive Order 11375, it's even so much better. Not that I expect any male chauvinists like yourself to understand the importance of that."

Parsons ignored her remarks and asked if any one of them was familiar with the history of Frederick Douglass, one of the most prominent Black abolitionists and reformers. Even though the guys knew the answer to Parsons' question — well, I could vouch that Kareem did — it was Tanya who responded:

"The Lion of Anacostia; birth name Frederick Augustus Washington Bailey; DOB about 1818; first African American to be nominated as Vice Presidential candidate to the first female candidate, Victoria Woodhull for the position of President of the United States of America; 1872. He is quoted as saying that he would unite with anybody to do right and with nobody to do wrong."

Parsons, referring to Tanya as the 'mystery lady', commended her for knowing her stuff, and sounded quite impressed with her. Anyway, he continued on the subject of Frederick Douglass:

"Douglass was reported as commenting, as you are most probably aware, on a frequently asked question,

> *. . . "**What shall we do with the Negro?** "**I have had but one answer from the beginning. Do nothing with us! Your doing***

with us has already played the mischief with us. Do nothing with us! If the apples will not remain on the tree of their own strength, if they are worm-eaten at the core, if they are early ripe and disposed to fall, let them fall! I am not for tying or fastening them on the tree in any way, except by nature's plan, and if they will not stay there, let them fall. And if the Negro cannot stand on his own legs, let him fall also. All I ask is, give him a chance to stand on his own legs! Let him alone!"

Kareem interjected:

"And, is it your conclusion that Mr. Douglass was, or would have been, averse to what affirmative action represents; 'crutches and wheel-chairs'?"

Parsons responded:

"Yes, sir, that is what I believe. It is my opinion that Frederick Douglass had a firm belief in the potentials, resourcefulness, and resilience of his fellow Blacks to meet and overcome all challenges. It is common knowledge to researchers of slavery and slave trading that the slaves who got sold quickly and fetched good money were those with the best qualities and attributes; good health, great physique, special skills and a whole lot more. Those were the same qualities that prevented many more of them from succumbing to the arduous sea voyage and the worst kinds of treatment from a number of slave owners.

"However, those who made it were tested to the limits of human endurance; they were favored by God and were the best of what Africa had to offer. You, their descendants, possess the best traits possible in anyone of African descent. Over the centuries and till today, Blacks (particularly

in this country) have proven themselves eligible to be counted among the ranks of the greatest scientists and inventors, entertainers, and sports men and women. I believe that was the basis of the confidence that Frederick Douglass had in his people.

"All that aside, I couldn't be more emphatic when I say that you cannot put the entire guilt of all that happened to your ancestors on all White men and all of their generations. The current generation of White folks is not guilty in any manner whatsoever for the sins of their ancestors. Not even all of their ancestors were guilty of crimes against Blacks. In any case, why should current and subsequent generations be held accountable, or made to pay for the mistakes of only some of their ancestors? This country belongs to all of us now — descendants of all races who paid dearly to build the most powerful nation on earth.

There is nothing wrong in helping the under-privileged of society and lifting one-another up when we are down. This, however, should not be done purely on the basis of appeasing a particular race because it is aggrieved, but on the basis that people of all races and colors and creeds will need the support of the government of this great nation from time to time.

Tell me something. Why are you not holding your kinfolk in Africa responsible for selling your ancestors — their own brothers and sisters? After all, the descendants of the perpetrators of the African end of the slave trade walk the streets of those African countries like superstars; still bathing in the influence and inherited ill-gotten wealth of their great-grandparents. Worse still, they also come over to this country to parade the streets as superstars. Why wouldn't you or haven't you been able to hold them accountable also?"

I listened to the exchange of views between Athiel, Tanya, Kareem and Parsons with keen interest. All of a sudden, the focus of the discussion on race and Black issues shifted to include religion as the basis for the White man's treatment of Blacks as inferior. Christianity, said Tanya, found no wrong with slavery.

She asked if Parsons had read the book, 'Narrative of the Life of Frederick Douglass, An American Slave' (1845). Not quite, Parsons responded:

There's a part of what Frederick Douglass said in that book about Christianity that is evident till this day — dealers in the bodies and souls of men erecting stands in the presence of the pulpit, and both sides mutually helping the other. He spoke of evil men giving blood-stained gold to support the Church, while the Church, in return, covers their evil business with the garb of Christianity.

According to Tanya, early Christian and Islamic teachings and writings about the supposed 'Curse of Ham' suggested and promoted, without any sound religious foundation, the belief that Black people are the descendants of Ham. The teachings and writings, she said, were deliberately interpreted to validate and encourage the enslavement of Africans by the West from as early as the 7th century. She suggested to Parsons that his views on Blacks might have been tainted by the Christian perspectives of his evangelist father.

Parsons replied:

In the first place, it is rather unfortunate that you could imagine or suggest that my father's views, or mine, were affected in any way by a supposed 'Curse of Ham'. Secondly, Ham was not cursed by his father, Noah, at all. The curse, as it were, was on Ham's son, Canaan. Thirdly, the fact that Ham and his descendants were reported to have settled in Egypt neither makes all Africans his descendants, nor does it grant a mandate to anyone to enslave another human being under the guise of helping to fulfill Noah's supposed curse. I have no idea what other curses exist in other parts of the world, the fact is that humans have always enslaved one another.

The portion of the Christian Bible to which Tanya was referring [Genesis 9:18-27] gave an account of an incident between Noah, his sons, and grandson. Even though the accounts in the Jewish Torah are significantly different, both versions of Scripture report an inappropriate act that involved Ham (Noah's last born) and Canaan (Noah's grandson by Ham) on a particular night when Noah fell into drunken sleep. When Noah came out of his drunken state and found out what had happened, he was said to have cursed his grandson, Canaan. Christianity and Islam erroneously teach that Ham, as opposed to Canaan, was cursed by Noah to forever serve his brothers and their descendants probably because of the close resemblance of his name to the Hebrew words that mean "black" and "hot". It is also taught that the descendants of Canaan were the occupants of Egypt and Ethiopia. However, Genesis 10:6 states Hams other sons, who were not cursed, as Egypt, Cush (Ethiopia) and Libya as being the ancestors of the people who bear their names. Anyway, utilizing the Curse of Ham as the basis for the enslavement of Blacks is generally regarded as one of the greatest misuses of the teachings of the Holy Bible.

Tanya responded rather delightedly:

Finally, we have a point on which we can both agree, Mr. Parsons. The 'Curse of Ham' was a pitiable excuse for the exploitation of the Black race by Whites. Then, could it be that your views are informed by the 'humanitarian' angle of the Rudyard Kipling message in 'The White Man's Burden'?

Parsons laughed and dismissed Tanya's statement as ridiculous. The Kipling tradition to which she referred suggested, more or less, that the West had the right to rule over and exploit second rate human beings – the class to which Blacks were classified. Kareem, who had been rather quiet throughout, decided to chip in at this point, and he had quite a bit to say:

In one of your lectures, you asked what else a White person must do to pay for the enslavement of Black people. Well, tell your White folks to stop their double standards. The last time I checked, when you receive stolen goods, or benefit from the proceeds of stolen goods or money, you are equally culpable of the crime of theft. You receive punishment just as the individual who stole. One doesn't need to go too far to find that out. Our jails are filled with the many indigent Blacks who bear testimony to that rule of law. These are young men and women whose crimes come nowhere close to what many top White business executives commit on a daily basis, the proceeds of which only qualify them for membership of high-dollar clubs around the world.

"White people accuse African leaders of egregious levels of corruption. The amounts that African leaders are accused of looting from their different countries are in the hundreds of millions of dollars. Since these huge amounts of money cannot be kept in any bank in their own countries, they are stashed in mostly White-owned financial institutions around the world. Mostly White business entities continue to benefit tremendously from stolen money and see no reason to put a stop to it. It is still my view that White people are interested only in those things that will serve their ultimate interest. Most of them are hypocrites. As a matter of fact, they encourage the looting of African nations by providing the villains in government anonymity and granting them a safe haven.

If White-owned financial institutions refuse to accept or stash ill-gotten wealth, or refuse to do business with any individuals or corporations who participate in keeping or using ill-acquired wealth, where would these corrupt African leaders keep their loot? This is the kind of action that might curtail their propensity to steal the wealth of their nations. If the West is sincere, they need to make it harder for leaders of developing nations to subject their people to new forms of enslavement. The way I see it now, nothing has changed much. What we have are just new players and new methods of doing the same old distasteful things.

For your information, Parsons, slavery is not yet over. Those of us in this room, as well as many others out there who feel the pain, know for a fact that the only thing that has changed is the method by and through which Whites enslave Blacks. The truth of the matter is that White people think they have done Blacks worldwide a huge favor which we must never forget. However, they resent the idea that we dare ask for equality. That is why your White relatives designed a system that will elevate whosoever it chooses, and never hesitates to pound the average Black man into the ground even when he tries so hard to rise. Discrimination against Black people will not go away for a long time."

Parsons interjected:

"Discrimination is a different thing. It has existed in our societies probably from when humans first trod the earth, and it still does. Even

184

within peoples of the same localities, race notwithstanding, it exists. Dis-crimination — or any other forms of prejudice — is not a Black or White thing. It's a human thing — common to all our global communities. Ter-rible kinds of prejudices and discrimination exist among people of the same race and ethnic groups all over the world.

"It would be correct to say that any kind of prejudice is an act or demonstration of ignorance; that is, having extremely very little or no knowledge whatsoever about an issue or subject. Ignorance, from that perspective therefore, has no racial or religious boundaries. Since almost all little children demonstrate no regard for race, religion or color at the early stages of their lives, it might be accurate to say that it is a bad habit that is inculcated in them either by parents or adults around them. In other words, none of you in this room was born feeling this way. We all grow up picking up both good and bad habits from our parents and from the kind of societies that have been built around us. I am not ready to debate that right now, but I cannot deny the fact that you are projecting feelings that are real; whichever way they were acquired, they are real. But, you are still missing the point."

Athiel asked Parsons what point he believed they were missing, and he continued to speak.

"Slavery was definitely not invented or started by the White man. Slavery existed within Africa long before the arrival of slave dealers from the Western world. Curse of Ham or not, the oldest records of human history attest to that. However, whichever way we wish to consider it, slavery was most certainly ended by the White man, at least as a business or practice in the Western world. Despite its tremendous economic benefits to their community, large numbers of white men and women protested and fought kinfolk to ensure the abolition of the evil practice of one man

owning another as property. One can comfortably draw the conclusion that the idea of abolishing slavery was favored by the majority of Whites because only numbers rule in a democratic society.

"In other words, there were more White people that were against slavery and interested in bringing it to an end than not. There is no doubt that there were various incidents of slave rebellion in different parts of America. However, there is no record that suggests slavery was officially abolished only and purely on account of those uprisings. No. The hue and cry against the enslavement of other humans came from most of the members of the same communities whose unscrupulous businesses benefited from slaves. The mere fact that this country succeeded in eventually abolishing slavery and slave trading officially, is an indication that a majority of the White-dominated population did not approve of slavery.

"How many young blacks today, probably even adults, know about or heard of William Wilberforce? Have you? What about John Brown; Eliza Parish Lovejoy; Lady Middleton; Granville Sharpe; and a host of other White male and female abolitionists?

"These were all White people who fought passionately to get their governments to bring slavery and the slave trade to an official end. William Wilberforce was a Member of the Parliament in the United Kingdom who devoted almost his entire life to the abolition of the slave trade and slavery.

"About the time I was in elementary school in West Africa, children used to sing about the heroic exploits of John Brown. John Brown, along with his sons, friends and sympathizers, fought against White slave owners to free and empower slaves. Unfortunately, he was caught and executed as a traitor to his own White community. While John Brown also lost two of his sons during the raid at Harper's Ferry in 1859, there were so many others who lost life and property on account of their invaluable efforts to end slavery and the slave trade over the years.

"In West Africa where slavery thrived, these men and women are regarded as heroes for their unparalleled contribution to end a practice that had devastated the lives of so many for so long. Here in America, very few African Americans even know who they were, and the significant contributions they made towards the Black cause. Personally, I think it's a shame that these great men and women who fought and died for your ancestors to gain freedom for themselves and their descendants are not given due recognition by Black communities worldwide. It's almost as if they all died in vain. Their heroic deeds are not even known or appreciated by the descendants of those they fought so hard to liberate. They are not celebrated in any way. Why?"

Athiel retorted:

"That is not an accurate statement, Mr. Parsons. How could you possibly suggest that their heroic deeds are not recognized?"

"Come on, mister, and in what way might that be? In the same way you celebrate Dr. Rev. Martin Luther King Jr.? Could the contributions of Martin Luther King have been anywhere close to the sacrifice of those White folks who not only freed his ancestors from bondage, but made it possible for him — and many before and after him — to obtain what was needed to take the struggle to the next level?"

Almost predictably, Tanya jumped back into the fray to ask if Parsons was suggesting that Dr. Martin Luther King Jr. was not deserving of his status and recognition in the civil rights struggle and consequent liberation of Blacks in America. This was one topic on which Tanya entertained no negativity. Dr. Martin Luther King Jr. was her hero, her icon.

Parsons answered that Dr. King will always be deserving of honor and recognition, as should Rosa Parks and others before and during the height of the Civil Rights movement. But, long before these equality and civil rights struggles, he said, there was the greater and near impossible battles for the abolition of the slave trade and slavery. Parsons stated that any acts which involve going up against the establishment and very powerful business interests will always represent an almost indomitable task. He described the journey of the African American on the road to freedom as one of those seemingly indomitable tasks that a handful of courageous men and women had to face and overcome. For the very powerful few, Parsons admitted, the business of slavery was extremely lucrative enough to ensure that Blacks were never allowed to rise beyond the level of 'beasts of burden'. But, even though the task seemed daunting – going up against powerful businesses and government laws that did not frown upon the ignoble practice – there were many men and women who did not balk at the challenges that lay ahead. While those battles may have been triggered by heroic and indomi-table Black men and women, Parsons maintained, they were championed by the majority of a courageous White race at different levels of society. According to him:

"A testament and celebration of the power of the collective will of different races, cultures, and colors — that is how we must see the victories along the road travelled by Black people from slavery to freedom. So, whether it is admitted or not, most of those White people you conveniently blame as the cause of your problems and for whom many of you harbor so

much intense dislike, helped in paving the way for later Black activists like Martin Luther King Jr. and others to follow. These are the same White people for whom your ancestors had so much admiration and respect. On two separate but equally important occasions, Frederick Douglass said of John Brown:

> *"... John Brown began the war that ended American slavery and made this a free Republic. His zeal in the cause of freedom was infinitely superior to mine. Mine was as the taper light; his was as the burning sun. I could live for the slave; John Brown could die for him."*

And, in a letter written to honor Harriet Tubman, Douglass also said:

> *"... The midnight sky and the silent stars have been the witnesses of your devotion to freedom and of your heroism. Excepting John Brown—of sacred memory—I know of no one who has willingly encountered more perils and hardships to serve our enslaved people than you have."*

With the way many Black people carry-on, one would be inclined to think that they brought the slave trade to an end and freed themselves from slavery. Do Black comments and sentiments these days ever reflect an iota of the gratitude that they owe White abolitionists and sympathizers who recognized all men as created in the image of God and thus deserving of respect and dignity? Did Africans — Egyptians — not enslave and maltreat Jews at some point in history thousands of years ago? Did Islamic

Jihadists from the Middle East not enslave and maltreat Africans at some point in history? Were the trade routes across the tortuous desert terrains any better that the voyages across the Atlantic? In both trades, millions of African slaves died while many suffered tremendously. A lot of Blacks in this country need to be advised to shove anger or bitterness aside and stand ready to seize advantage of any opportunities that are available to them."

Athiel cut in angrily:

"It is insulting and downright ignorant and insensitive of you, or anyone else, to describe the cries of Black men and women against visible injustice and palpable suffering as carrying-on. Watch your utterances, Parsons.

Parsons responded with equal anger and defiance:

"There's injustice in every society all over the world, mister, even among people of the same ethnicity. And, if you want to talk about equality, that is something that no government on the face of the earth can offer anyone. You guys need to either wake up or grow up, really. Plus, why conduct this inquisition if you are not ready for straight talk? Some abolitionists lost their lives and loved ones, while many lost property and reputation. That is an incontrovertible fact. My father left the comfort of Western civilization to serve in Africa. He saw no color when he married my mother, just another human being with whom he fell in love.

"What your actions and sentiments show is ingratitude; ingratitude for the sacrifice of good people who happened to be White but drew no difference in skin color whenever they have fought to preserve the dignity and equality of Black people. They have descendants too, you know. How do you expect them to feel when you make uncomplimentary sweeping statements about all White folks, in total disregard of the high moral integrity

demonstrated by their ancestors in a world where morality, as we know it today, was differently defined?

By the time I got the audio cassette tape from Kareem, I had established close rapport with Thomas Parsons. This had given me an opportunity to ask questions on wide-ranging issues. There was no doubt that he had battled internal conflicts as do most of us, but probably more so because he was bi-racial. He confessed that he had struggled to find identity in a world that drew very harsh lines along the boundaries of race, color and religion. However, regarding Thomas Parsons' and his views, I have had to ask myself a few questions. Had he chosen the perspective of the side of the family tree that favored him the most as his way of resolving his internal conflicts? In that regard, can one tell by his views which side of the Black and White family tree influenced him more? And, was that influence mostly positive or negative?

My father always said that the sensible and truly educated Black person must understand that he cannot become a White person by merely learning Western culture, or just by acquiring enlightenment in the Western fashion. A Black person must know for a fact that God did not create him or her inferior to any other human. Each human being must learn to find out how to unleash the enormous spiritual potential that lies below skin color. Life is about understanding why you are who you are, why you are where you are, and where you really should or could be.

God's wisdom and guidance are available to all men and women whose self-imposed ways do not constitute a hindrance to themselves. If you have great difficulty climbing to the top of the mountain of your potentials, you need to find out in what ways you might be hindering yourself. God does not hinder anyone.

IN CONCLUSION

With diligence, I pored over all the notes and works of Thomas Parsons (the Black White Man) and my dad. Most of the details were verifiable, but a few I could not confirm for reasons of the logistics involved. The passion and views expressed by the different players are still as relevant today as they were many years ago, even though a lot has changed. Before the recent passing of my dad, he had drawn my attention to events happening in different parts of the world and the pattern of reaction in this country.

In January 2010, a 7.0 earthquake (which included at least fifty-two aftershocks that registered about 5.0 on the Richter scale) hit the country of Haiti. The horrific event took approximately 320,000 lives, injured more than 300,000 and left over one million people homeless. During and after the disaster, my dad had paid very close attention to the rescue efforts, the financial and logistics support of various governments, and the contributions of private and corporate entities to cope with the aftermath of the catastrophic event. Curiously, he noted, the input of rich Black nations and extremely wealthy Black individuals all over the world was minimal. A couple of Haiti's local celebrities even made a bold bid to take advantage of the 200-year unparalleled disaster to advance their personal interests, above the pain and suffering of the people.

Most noteworthy, my dad observed, and probably greater than any contribution made by governments, corporations or individuals , was the personal commitment and invaluable effort and role played by Hollywood actor, Sean Penn – a White man. That young man, dad said, had joined the ranks of many other White men and women like him, who have been known to abandon the comforts and convenience offered by their personal lifestyles to take up the unglamorous jobs and roles of caring for the helpless and down-trodden of this world, regardless of their color, race or creed.

In another ongoing development, he told me how happy he was to read about the efforts and huge progress of Hollywood actor, George Clooney, in his quest to prevent possible genocide in the African country of Sudan. Unfortunately, in a world where sensational news is the only good news in mass media, the good news about George Clooney's success so far constituted … no news. In dad's opinion, a detailed analysis of the disaster that George Clooney's proactive efforts, commitment, and foresight would prevent in the Sudan should have been given more extensive coverage. He was toiling earnestly and tirelessly to prevent a humanitarian crisis in the Sudan that could be equal to, or greater than, the 1994 genocide in Rwanda that took almost one million lives.

So far, it looked more likely than not that South Sudan would gain independence without a bloodbath – mostly thanks to Clooney utilizing his considerable influence to draw worldwide attention to the potential crisis. Again, dad said, this was another White man spending time, money and energy and risking his life to ensure that young and old Black men and women on the African continent have a much better future to look forward to. Why is this situation (and many other similar situations on the African continent) of little or no concern to African American leaders?

In the African Democratic Republic of the Congo, he continued, where the death toll has exceeded six million Black men, women and children since 1998, the main advocates of a solution to the mayhem are also mostly White people – Ben Affleck and Cindy McCain, supported by other White folks. The deplorable situation in this scenic African nation has been aptly described as a Nightmare in Heaven.

According to Gregory Stanton (US state Dept. 1992-1999) – President, Genocide Watch, "There's a pattern to genocide. It's like a hurricane. You can see it coming." In essence, and as George Clooney is trying to prove with the South Sudan situation, terrible humanitarian disasters can be prevented if there are enough people in the world who truly care about one another across boundaries of race, color or creed.

Maurice Carney, Co-Founder & Executive Director, Friends of the Congo asks, "Is there a global consensus that exists that says it is okay for six million Black people to die in the heart of Africa and for us to be silent?" He says, and records offer support, that hundreds of thousands of women are systematically raped in the Congo in the name of war. His views are backed by Anneke Van Woudenberg, Sr. Reseacher, Human Rights Watch. She states that policy makers cannot claim they do not know these facts. Congo, she says, is one of the worst places in the world to be a woman or a girl. Anneke tells the story of a fifteen year old girl who was kept in a pit by soldiers as a sex slave and raped in turn for three months by any and every soldier – even after it was discovered that she had gotten pregnant. The teenage girl had to live in the same pit for two weeks with the body of a friend that had been killed and dumped there.

Nita Evele, of Congo Global Action, describes rape as one of the most lethal weapons of war in that region. Apart from other motives, it is a calculated move to destabilize the community. According to her, raping the women of entire villages in front of their children, their husbands and neighbors ensures that the community is broken completely.

Claver Pashi, Executive Director, DR Congo Forum, says that "people are being reduced to the level of a non-human so that they cannot think, so that they can feel powerless and hopeless, so that they can give up."

So, who are these people who perpetrate such evil? They are none other than Black people – perpetrating unthinkable evil on their fellow Black men and women and children in these modern times. Yaa-Lengi Ngemi, Author, *Genocide in the Congo (Zaire)*, asks, "Are we going to wait for twenty more years before somebody stops this holocaust?"

Howard French of the New York Times and Associate Professor, Columbia Graduate School of Journalism, states with a lot of concern, "There is something wrong. There is something wrong with us – in the way we think of Africa. The situation has warranted no sustained and enterprising reporting from the media of the world, and obtained no great purchase on the popular imagination, even with millions of people dead."

Ben Affleck, Cindy McCain and other concerned citizens of the world are asking for support and the full implementation Bill PL 109-456. The bill was sponsored by President Barack Obama and US Secretary of State Hilary Clinton, when both of them were serving in the US Senate. The Bill calls for different forms of interventions and solutions to the Congo disaster.

'Crisis in the Congo – Uncovering the Truth', is the title of a shocking documentary of hell-on-earth, made by www.friendsofthecongo.org and available on You Tube.

According to my dad, in this age or in the past, it is unimaginable that White folks would keep quiet over the continuing massacre of over six million men, women and children of their own kind.

As usual, some Black folks might be quick to suggest that the problems in the Congo are being caused by unscrupulous White-owned businesses seeking to benefit from the Congo's vast natural resources. While that may be so, both of us wondered what actions were being taken by African American leaders to protect the interests of our kin in Africa.

With the obvious exception of Oprah Winfrey (who has enriched the lives and future of many in South Africa), Alicia Keys and possibly a couple of others, it is difficult to point out any other influential Black organization or African Americans who have taken an interest in the plight of young men and women on their continent of origin. For Oprah's bold and unusual move, dad and I recalled how much flak she got from the African American community in particular. In characteristic manner, she brushed off all attacks and remained focused on what she felt happy and personally compelled to do.

Not too long ago, dad said he had watched a news story that Sandra Bullock had adopted a Black baby. Even though other White superstars like Madonna and Angelina Jolie had also done the same, he said that he was piqued by a comment made on television, by a Black lady, about the Sandra Bullock adoption. Her problem with the adoption, the Black lady stated, was that the successful White actress would be unable to raise the Black child in the culture of his race.

What culture, dad asked? Would it have been better to deprive that Black child the love and opportunities he would get from a person of Sandra Bullock's stature, just because he might grow up in an atmosphere devoid of hip-hop music and a 'doctrine of the separation of colors'?

For as long as that child, and others like him, can be raised to redefine themselves and their values outside of just being a color, they would be on the right path towards being better citizens of the world indeed. According to my dad, achieving a more cohesive and powerful future human community will be impossible if what we have to pass on is a legacy of hate and distrust.

We see a world community that is slowly moving beyond the issues of prejudices to asking what any man or woman has to offer human society. In other words, how relevant can you be to your immediate and larger human society? Humankind is being driven towards developing a culture of excellence over and above age-old traditions and cultures that should merely serve as a remembrance of where we all came from. In the emerging world, relevance will be the new smart.

Slavery and slave trading may be officially over in the sense of its lawfulness. However, dad stated, enslavement is another issue altogether. Enslavement, which he suggested is now narrowly substituted with the word 'addiction', has been around from the dawn of humankind and will remain till the 'end of days'. Almost every man or woman is enslaved to one thing or another – anger, envy, greed, jealousy, food, drugs, sex and a host of other things. In other words, every one of us is a slave to the emotions, vices or habits that control our daily existence. From these, no laws can be made to free any man or woman, except we free ourselves.

Former President Bill Clinton, former British Prime Minister Tony Blair and leaders of some other Western nations apologized for the despicable act of slavery, dad noted. Has any of the culpable African nations who participated very actively in the slave trade ever rendered an apology, he asked?

Honestly speaking, the mindset in the African countries that practiced, and still practice, slavery has not changed much. They still cannot come to terms with why the practice and lucrative business has now become so abominable. This is not the kind of mind set that is ever likely to accept responsibility or apologize for playing an 'evil' role in what, to them, was simply part of a long-standing culture and a common business practice.

My dad and I were agreed on the fact that African American leaders do not help the situation by not 'pushing' African nations and leaders for accountability and an apology for their very active role in slave trading. Africa is an extremely rich continent whose nations now have full control of their resources. I truly believe it is time for African American leaders to strongly urge leaders of all African nations that participated in slavery to join hands with known Western entities who were involved in slavery or the slave trade, to contribute to programs that will help fund and develop opportunities for under-privileged Black descendants of slaves around the world. That would be a more honorable thing to do, and it would go a very long way towards healing old wounds.

Unfortunately, almost all African nations have bad leadership and their people even suffer much more than they ever did under colonialists. The wealth of African nations is being plundered by their leaders more than any colonial government ever did. The majority of Africans have never had less hope for their future, or suffered more oppression and brutality than in the hands of their own people who eventually become leaders.

It has always been fashionable for the Black man to blame all of his problems on the White man, dad had said. After all, many Blacks have been convinced to the effect that it was the White man's venture into Africa that complicated the life of the simple Black man who was just minding his own life and business on the Dark Continent.

Well, he said, that was what happened and there is nothing that anyone living today can do about what happened hundreds of years in the past. Whether we blame it on greed, ignorance, or expansionism, what happened in the past is now irrelevant except we can utilize the experiences to chart a positive way forward into the future. The daunting fact is that we must deal with whatever we have all inherited as best as we can. Therefore, regardless of how or why the West came into Africa, the earlier the Black man stops seeing the White man, as opposed to himself, as the only reason for his woes, the better it will be for him and everybody.

Regardless of how or why the West came into Africa, dad always said, the White man is still playing more than a key role in African issues and affairs, while most African leaders have done no more than constitute themselves into stumbling blocks to the welfare of their own people.

Who is always the first at the scene of any major disaster in Africa, remains at the scene, and is the last to leave the scene? The answer is simple – Western governments, Western companies, and both small and major Western philanthropists. In some cases, some leaders have been known to prevent or disrupt aid from reaching their own people.

Even when it is either about donating medicines to combat disease or educational materials to improve the chances of survival of young Black children in a competitive world, African leaders remain lackadaisical to available aid from Western governments and both private and corporate philanthropists. On many occasions, these resources intended for the needy, are misappropriated for personal financial benefits.

With the exception of Black philanthropists in the United States of America, how many Black philanthropists can Africa boast of, even though many African leaders and businessmen individually possess more wealth than many small nations on the globe?

Generally speaking, dad said more times than I can remember, the Black man or woman must start taking full responsibility, as every human being should, for his or her life so that they can start shaping their individual or collective destiny.

Frederick Douglass once said **"A true patriot is a lover of his country who rebukes and does not excuse its sins."**

Along those same lines, my dad would say that a true and genuine person is a lover of his people who rebukes and does not excuse their failings and shortcomings.

In dad's opinion, there are two major issues in race relations that will tarry for a while, but slowly improve, as we carry on into the future; residual racism from Whites and residual anger from Blacks. No number of laws can be promulgated to cure these endemic problems. Despite individual and government effort, reparations or affirmative action, residual racism will certainly not vanish overnight while residual anger will rise to the surface every now and then to threaten great achievements in race relations.

However, there is no problem on the face of the earth that cannot be overcome. He believes that we must all make a conscious effort to recognize and appreciate the uniqueness of each race or group and what they can contribute to the overall well-being of the entire human race. Dad wrote in his memoirs:

"There are so many people in history who have sacrificed so much for the freedom and equality of all men. Whether past or present, there are many people of different races who made significant sacrifices to promote freedom and equality for all men and women. There are still many today who remain watchful and continue to serve the cause of humanity worldwide. No amount of animosity should ever be allowed to diminish the contributions of decent, God-fearing men and women who fight tirelessly for an end to the horrible treatment and unimaginable suffering of the weak and less privileged in the global human community.

"It is in memory of all those of our ancestors – Black, White, Red, and Brown – who fought and died for the freedom and liberties we enjoy today, that we must let go of our pain and be willing to participate in the healing process. We must help the ghosts from our past find rest by not invoking them as often as we do. The first step must be to find forgiveness within our hearts for one another. A great and peaceful global human community cannot be built or sustained on a foundation of bitterness, distrust and apathy."

Let's play a little game, my dad used to say when I was a kid. Very quickly, I learnt the difference between "let's go play a game" (a physical sport) and "let's play a game" (a mental sport). Even though the mental sport varied, some of the games were reinforced more than others. The ones most often repeated included the magic of numbers (to spark and sustain my interest in mathematics), learning simple ways to remember planets in the solar system (Men Very Easily Make Jugs Serve Useful New Purposes – with all the first letters representing the names of the planets), and the heroes to who we owe a debt of gratitude for the freedoms that we enjFor every white abolitionist he named, I had to name a Black counterpart or vice versa. Also, for every name that was mentioned, a brief description of their lives and work had to be given.

Many years later, I recall asking, "Are we including living heroes like Reverend Jesse Jackson and John Lewis, or are we restricted only to the dead?" The old man laughed and said, "That's alright, Junior. Both living and dead, and you are already two ahead. For your two, I will start with William Wilberforce and John Brown". And so, we would begin our little game, sometimes with support from friends or family.

William Wilberforce (1759-1833) – Caucasian. He was a British politician, Member of Parliament, philanthropist, and prominent leader of abolitionist movement. In 1787, he teamed up anti-slave-trade group including Thomas Clarkson, Hannah More, Granville Sharp, and Charles Middleton. Wilberforce headed the parliamentary campaign against the British slave trade for twenty-six years until the passage of the Slave Trade Act of 1807. Even though he resigned from Parliament due to ill health in 1826, he led the campaign that led to the Slavery Abolition Act 1833, which abolished slavery in most of the British Empire. William Wilberforce died on 29th July, 1833; one month after Parliament passed the Slavery Abolition Act that gave all slaves in the British Empire their freedom.

John Brown (1800–1859) – Caucasian. He was an American abolitionist who advocated and practiced armed insurrection as a means to abolish all slavery. John Brown led the Pottawatomie Massacre in 1856 in Bleeding Kansas and the unsuccessful raid at Harpers Ferry in 1859, which historians agree escalated tensions that a year later led to secession and the American Civil War.

Brown demanded violent action in response to Southern aggression. Dissatisfied with the pacifism encouraged by the organized abolitionist movement, he was quoted to have said "These men are all talk. What we need is action - action!" The raid he led on the federal armory at Harpers Ferry was intended to arm slaves with weapons from the arsenal, but the attack failed. Brown was captured, tried for treason to the state of Virginia, and executed by hanging in Charles Town, Virginia. According to Harriet Tubman, **"[H]e done more in dying, than 100 men would in living."** He is sometimes heralded as a heroic martyr and a visionary and sometimes vilified as a madman and a terrorist.

Harriet Tubman (born **Araminta Ross**, c. 1820–1913 of Ashanti, Ghana lineage) – Negro. This was a female African-American abolitionist, humanitarian, and Union spy during the U.S. Civil War. After escaping from captivity, she made thirteen missions to rescue over seventy slaves using the network of antislavery activists and safe houses known as the Underground Railroad.

When the American Civil War began, Tubman worked for the Union Army, first as a cook and nurse, and then as an armed scout and spy. The first woman to lead an armed expedition in the war, she guided the raid on the Combahee River, which liberated more than seven hundred slaves. Despite the best efforts of the slaveholders, Tubman was never captured – and neither were the fugitives she guided. Years later, she told an audience: **"I was conductor of the Underground Railroad for eight years, and I can say what** most conductors can't say — I never ran my train off the track and I never lost a passenger."

Harriet Tubman died in 1913, and was buried with military honors at Fort Hill Cemetery in Auburn. In 1944 the United States Maritime Commission launched the *SS Harriet Tubman*, its first Liberty ship ever named for a black woman.

Frederick Douglass (born **Frederick Augustus Washington Bailey**, 1818–1895) – Negro. He was an American abolitionist, editor, orator, author, statesman and reformer. Called "The Sage of Anacostia" and "The Lion of Anacostia", Douglass is one of the most prominent figures in African American history and a formidable public presence. Douglass was nominated to run as the Vice Presidential candidate on the Equal Rights Party ticket alongside Victoria Woodhull, the first female to run for President of the United States, in the 1872 election. He was a firm believer in the equality of all people, whether black, female, Native American, or recent immigrant. Frederick Douglass died in his adopted hometown of Washington, D.C.

Granville Sharpe (1735-1813) – Caucasian. An abolitionist and author often called "the father of the Cause" by contemporaries. His interest in the plight of Africans in England began with his encounter in 1765 with Jonathan Strong, a slave from Barbados, beaten and abandoned in London by his master who later attempted to kidnap him and send him back to the Caribbean. Sharp successfully defended Strong's rights and those of other Africans as well. He was a founder member of the Committee for Effecting the Abolition of the African Slave Trade.

John Newton (1725-1807) – Caucasian. Most famous as the author of the hymn "Amazing Grace", Newton captained two Liverpool slave ships in his youth. He embraced religion during this time and in 1755 gave up the sea for the church. He later developed deep regrets over his involvement in the slave trade and supported William Wilberforce in his abolition campaign. He gave evidence to the Privy Council hearings on the trade and wrote a tract supporting abolition, Thoughts upon the African Slave Trade (1787).

Ottawa Ignatius Sancho (1729-1780) – Negro. He was born into slavery on a ship bound from Africa to the Americas. Brought to London as a young boy, he worked as a child slave for two sisters at Greenwich. He was named Sancho by them after Don Quixote's squire. The sisters did not believe in educating slaves but Sancho taught himself to read and write. His collected letters, which were influential in championing abolition and condemning the slave trade, were later published.

Thomas Fowell Buxton (1786-1845) – Caucasian. British Member of Parliament, abolitionist and social reformer, he was asked by William Wilberforce to continue the campaign against slavery in Parliament when Wilberforce retired. He founded, with Wilberforce, the Society for the Mitigation and Gradual Abolition of Slavery in 1823. He became vice-president of the Anti-Slavery Society, and in 1839 he established the Society for the Extinction of the Slave Trade and the Civilization of Africa.

Olaudah Equiano (1745-1797) – Negro. He wrote that he was enslaved as a child and bought by an English Naval Captain who named him Gustavus Vassa after a famous Swedish King. Equiano later fought in the Seven Years War as an Able Seaman in the British Navy... bought his freedom and worked as a hairdresser in London. He became the defender of black interests, trying to prevent people from being kidnapped and sold into slavery, some-times working with other black Londoners known as "The Sons of Africa". Appointed commissary in the scheme to send hundreds of London's black poor to Sierra Leone, he left after exposing official corruption and ill-treatment of the migrants.

John Woolman (1720-1772) – Caucasian. A travel-ling Quaker speaker, he was one of the earliest objectors to slave ownership and came to England from New Jersey in 1772 to gain support from English Quakers. After receiving this in London he set off for York. Woolman refused to use any slave plantation produce, including fabric dyes such as indigo, and so wore completely white clothes. John Wool-man later died of smallpox.

Joseph Sturge (1793-1859) – Caucasian. He was a Quaker abolitionist, co-founded the Agency Committee of the Anti-Slavery Society in 1831, which pressed for immediate and entire emancipation. His sister, Sophia Sturge (1795-1845) was a co-founder of the Birmingham Ladies Society for the Relief of Negro Slaves.

Kobna Ottobah Cugoano (about 1757 - unknown) – Negro, was born in Ajumako, Gold Coast (modern day Ghana), sold into slavery at the age of 13 and transported to work on a plantation in Grenada. He was a friend of Equiano and one of the first African-Britons actively engaged in the campaign for the abolition of slavery. His book, *Thoughts and Sentiments on the Evil and Wicked Traffic of the Slavery and Commerce of the Human Species*, published in 1787, rejected all arguments that supported African enslavement. Cugoano was baptized in the name of **John Stuart** in 1773 in London. Nothing is known of his life after 1791.

Thomas Clarkson (1760-1846) – Caucasian. He was a leading abolitionist who, as founder and main researcher for the Committee for Effecting the Abolition of the African Slave Trade, travelled the country investigating the conditions on slave ships and interviewing sailors and ship's surgeons, often at personal risk. Clarkson wrote many books and pamphlets on the slave trade as well as travelling all over the country to promote the campaign through boycotts and petitions.

William Roscoe (1753-1831) - Caucasian, was historian and writer, described as "Liverpool's greatest citizen", was MP for the city from 1806-7. He founded the Liverpool branch of the Anti-Slavery Society, helped to establish the African Institute and campaigned in parliament to ban the slave trade, despite violent protests against him.

Zachary Macaulay (1768-1838) – Caucasian. An abolitionist and campaigner, he had been a bookkeeper on a Jamaican plantation and became very involved in the campaign to abolish the slave trade. Macaulay was a leading member of a group of Evangelical Anglicans, including William Wilberforce, who campaigned for social reforms such as the abolition of the slave trade. In 1790 Macaulay went to Sierra Leone, to help emancipated slaves from Britain's former American colonies who had gone to create a new settlement there, and came home on a slave ship to gather facts about conditions for the abolitionist campaign.

James Farmer (1920–1999) – Negro. He was a prominent Black civil rights activist who was one of the "big 6" leaders of the American civil rights movement of the 1950s and 1960s. Along with a group of students, he co-founded the Committee of Racial Equality in 1942, later known as the Congress of Racial Equality (CORE), an organization whose aim was to end racial segregation in America through active nonviolence. He was the organization's first leader, serving as the national chairman from

1942 to 1944. In 1961, while working for the NAACP at the time, he was reelected as the national director of CORE, at a time when the civil rights movement was gaining worldwide recognition.

Medgar Wiley Evers (1925–1963) – Negro, was an African American civil rights activist from Decatur Mississippi who was murdered by a member of the Ku Klux Klan. In 1943, at the age of 17, Evers enlisted in the army with his older brother. He fought in the European Theatre of WWII and was honorably discharged in 1945 as a Sergeant. He helped to organize the boycott of service stations that denied blacks use of their restrooms. The boycotters distributed bumper stickers with the slogan "Don't Buy Gas Where You Can't Use the Restroom." He became a prominent black leader and therefore vulnerable to attack.

Earl Grey – Caucasian. As Foreign Secretary and Leader of the House of Commons, **Charles Grey**, (Earl Grey) (1764-1845) was responsible for seeing the act abolishing the African slave trade through parliament. In 1833, as Prime Minister, Earl Grey led the government in enacting the law that was to end slavery in the Caribbean.

Elijah Parish Lovejoy (1802 - 1837) - Caucasian, an American Presbyterian minister, journalist, abolitionist and newspaper editor who was murdered by a pro-slavery mob in Alton, Illinois for his abolitionist views. He had a deep religious upbringing … attended the Princeton Theological Seminary and became an ordained Presbyterian preacher.

In May 1836, he was run out of town by his opponents after he chastised a judge who had chosen not to charge individuals linked to a mob lynching of a free black man. He supported the emancipation of slaves, to the disapproval of many Missourians. On November 7, 1837, pro-slavery partisans congregated …. Lovejoy was shot with a shotgun loaded with slugs and was hit five times; … Afterwards, Lovejoy was considered a martyr by the abolition movement.

Martin Luther King, Jr., (January 15, 1929-April 4, 1968) – Negro, was born Michael Luther King, Jr., but later had his name changed to Martin. His grandfather began the family's long tradition as pastors of the Ebenezer Baptist Church in Atlanta, Georgia where he also served from 1960 until his death as co-pastor with his father. In 1957 he was elected president of the Southern Christian Leadership Conference, an organization formed to provide new leadership for the growing civil rights movement. The ideals for this organization he took from Christianity; its operational techniques from Gandhi.

In the eleven-year period between 1957 and 1968, King traveled over six million miles and spoke over twenty-five hundred times, appearing wherever there was injustice, protest, and action. King wrote five books and numerous articles. He directed the peaceful march on Washington, D.C., of 250,000 people to whom he delivered his address,

"1 Have a Dream", he conferred with President John F. Kennedy and campaigned for President Lyndon B. Johnson; he was arrested upwards of twenty times and assaulted at least four times; he was awarded five honorary degrees; was named Man of the Year by *Time* magazine in 1963; and became the symbolic leader of American blacks and a world figure. At the age of thirty-five, Martin Luther King, Jr., was the youngest man to have received the Nobel Peace Prize. On the evening of April 4, 1968, he was assassinated.

The following piece, rounded up at the end by my dad, was written by Thomas Parsons – the Black White Man. From my understanding, it was the last manuscript Parsons handed over to him just before he died. It is my opinion that this will serve as a fitting conclusion to this book:

"Particularly with the benefit of hindsight, the Black community really needs to appreciate the context behind the statement made by Booker T. Washington, a former slave whose life and history has long been a source of inspiration for all those whose ancestors were taken out of Africa. In his book, 'Up from Slavery', he wrote,

"**...I have long since ceased to cherish any spirit of bitterness against the Southern white people on account of the enslavement of my race. No one section of our country was wholly responsible for its introduction... Having once got its tentacles fastened on to the economic** and social life of the Republic, it was no easy matter for the country to relieve itself of the institution. Then, when we rid ourselves of prejudice, or racial feeling, and look facts in the face, we must acknowledge that, notwith-standing the cruelty and moral wrong of slavery, the ten million Negroes inhabiting this country, who themselves or whose ancestors went through the school of Ameri-can slavery, are in a stronger and more hopeful condition, materially, intellectually, morally, and religiously, than is true of an equal number of black people in any other portion of the globe. ...This I say, not to justify slavery – on the other hand, I condemn it as an institution, as we all know that in America it was established for selfish and financial reasons, and not from a missionary motive – but to call attention to a fact, and to show how Providence so often uses men and institutions to accomplish a purpose. When persons ask me in these days how, in the midst of what sometimes seem hopelessly discouraging conditions, I can have such faith in the future of my race in this coun-try, I remind them of the wilderness through which and out of which, a good Providence has already led us... ."

Let us consider the case of freed slaves who actually went back to Africa to settle in countries like Sierra Leone, Gabon and Liberia. In no way, shape or form could their achievements or that of their descendants, be measured or matched against the giant strides taken by those who, through foresight, chose to stay behind. Our ancestors made a decision to bear the pain and the humiliation in order to gain a strategic foothold for their offspring in the most powerful nations on earth. They are around no more, but our ancestors certainly knew what they were doing. The beauty of it all is that they succeeded. Shall we now squander their wonderful legacy?

In the long run, African Americans are numbered among those who influence the affairs of men and women of all colors and races all over the world, and in all fields of human endeavor. While some may say that the battle has not been completely won, there is a need to realize that the 'campaign' has been successful.

Overall, even though some might disagree, the worst is over for Black citizens of Western nations. That is, of course, only as far as they would not allow their residual anger with White folks become a distraction of sorts. Without a doubt, a small percentage of racially-motivated crimes and some forms of prejudice will occur from time to time – prompted by traces of the bad old times, or just part of basic human nature. But, at some point in time in the future, hopefully sooner than later, racially-motivated crimes will no longer be the norm. Will prejudice-related crimes go away permanently? I do not think so. This is based on the fact that there will always be ignorant human beings in every shade of color, race, or creed. Ignorance will always breed fear, suspicion, and other base animal instincts – nothing good.

As far as the Black community goes, unfortunately, the worst is developing. Something is happening that is threatening to destroy the accomplishments for which our ancestors suffered and labored. Black people, in this nation and in other parts of the world, are killing themselves faster and in greater numbers than any White men ever did. You say that the White man kills and hates you because he is racist and prejudiced against your skin color and your kind. What is your excuse for hating, distrusting and killing your own brothers and sisters – members of your own families? Were the struggles and sacrifices of decent men and women, Black and White, made so that Black people, in this country in particular, gain the freedom to kill and maim one another? It is my hope that current and future generations of Blacks will be able to build upon the legacy – the courage, tenacity and history-making achievements – of great Black men and women who were once terribly yoked by the scourge of slavery.

There is no greater enemy to any man or woman than the enemy that lies within. As it stands, there is no greater enemy to the Black community than Blacks themselves – in this country and in other parts of the world. In what seems like a recurring nightmare, it seems that Black people just cannot stop killing and selling-out one another – whether on their home continent or in any other communities around the world.

It should be quite obvious that the problems facing the Black race, in general, are more profound than Black leaders care to imagine, see or admit. Unfortunately, I have heard from a number of Black folks that telling one another the truth is not a tradition that is generally embraced in Black communities. Therefore, if it is the high percentage of poverty that has continued to exacerbate the problems of Black people, then the issue of poverty needs to be addressed most urgently and more comprehensively. If a lack of education has contributed to the problems, then the subject of education must be vigorously addressed on a global scale – even encompassing people of all races or colors. Whatever constitutes the problem – greed, deprivation or exploitation, African American leaders need to be at the forefront of global efforts that are being made to find lasting solutions to the problems of Blacks worldwide. They must join hands with leaders of other races to address issues that prevent the cohesion and advancement of the global human community. Attitudes and practices, such as are emerging locally in this country, can only serve to impede growth within the Black community and the United States of America as a whole.

Those who must be leaders must have the clear vision that only comes from a healthy mind and spirit. A clear vision, however, cannot be achieved if those who would lead refuse to allow old wounds to heal and old ghosts to rest. If the leaders have no desire to allow themselves to heal, or do not know how to go about finding ways to heal, how can they provide the kind of healthy leadership that will enrich the lives of those who look up to them? At the same time, those who must follow can only follow effectively if they are also healthy in mind and spirit. Altogether, they cannot afford to continue reliving the horrors and nightmares of the past at the expense of dreams and possibilities of a more beautiful tomorrow.

Admittedly from a casual overview, one could almost draw the conclusion that what some Blacks seek most from the White man is enablement and support to undermine and destroy his own kind. Sadly, there will always be an abundance of unscrupulous people – in every race or color – who will gladly enable those who are so inclined, and even participate, in any and all clandestine propositions.

From an official standpoint, slavery and slave-trading may have been abolished all over the world, but regardless of race or color, many of us still remain enslaved to one thing or another – ideas, traditions, personal "demons" or addictions, and even fellow humans. Enslavement, ultimately, is more mental than physical. It has so much more to do with what happens to, and in, one's mind than the body. In effect, this means that a man or woman may still remain enslaved even long after the fetters of slavery are gone, depending on the state of his or her mind.

Therefore, except a person is ready to be free, no one can free him or her from any kind of bondage. Bad people may hold your body captive, but they must never be allowed to hold your mind captive. That is where your strength lies. You must protect your mind always..."

The foregoing submission by Thomas Parsons, while obviously debatable, contained many points or truths that need to be addressed.

This world, this earth, is more interconnected than many people care to imagine. At the end of the day, a service rendered for someone else and for the world in which we all live, is a service rendered to oneself.

As Thomas Parsons once said to me, the longer it takes for deeply-rooted issues of anger and betrayal to be uprooted and cast away, the longer it will take for those who, by a special providence, have become Princes and Princesses of the most powerful nations on earth to heal in order to achieve their higher calling. The next step for the Black community must be to find the healthy and uplifting strength and peace of mind that come automatically with forgiveness, unity and harmony with one's fellow men and women throughout the world.

Let the healing begin.

BIBLIOGRAPHY

Up From Slavery: An Autobiography, by Booker T. Washington (1901)

The Holy Bible

Narrative of the Life of Frederick Douglass, by Frederick Douglass (1845)

ABOUT THE AUTHORS

Vou Pam is both an author and a publisher. This is another of her collaborative works with author D.R.B. Tarr. She is also President of a non-profit organization, Noble Spirits Worldwide Inc., which advocates a re-definition of our values, beliefs, and general lifestyles as a necessary approach towards building more well-informed and tolerant human communities throughout the world. The organization seeks to promote global cooperation at community levels and the eradication of all kinds of prejudice. For more information, visit www.noblespiritsworld.com

Vou Pam is of Bermudian, Portuguese, and African descent. She is the daughter of an acclaimed author of children's books. She has lived in Beijing, China and in Dubai, UAE and is widely travelled. She currently resides in the United States with her family.

D. R. B. Tarr is a businessman and author. As a result of particularly significant life experiences, he has been involved in a unique type of research of world religions for over thirty years. His business and religious pursuits have taken him to different countries in Europe, the Middle and Far East, different parts of Africa, the Caribbean and Canada. He is the Founder of a non-profit organization established to enable and support the elderly and the disabled. D. R. B. Tarr currently resides in the United States.

www.ingramcontent.com/pod-product-compliance
Lightning Source LLC
Chambersburg PA
CBHW030133180626
46812CB00002B/671